Lithium

by F D G Ferrabee

First published by Lulu Books 2023

ISBN 978-1-304-854117

Edition number 1 – December 2023

This is a work of fiction. Unless otherwise indicated, all the names, characters, businesses, places, events and incidents in this book are either the product of the author's imagination or used in a fictitious manner. Any resemblance to actual persons, living or dead, or actual events is purely coincidental. Nothing should be inferred. No animals were hurt in the creation of this work.

Table of Contents

Lithium

Prelude – Solitude

Appreciative Inquiry

Pioneered by the wonderfully named David Cooperrider in the last century. It claims to build on the work of the golf and tennis Olympian, Frederick Wilmslow Taylor, who arguably created the concept of commercial organisations in the late 1800s. Cooperrider and his mentor Suresh Srivastva suggested we take a more positive approach to innovation and continuous improvement. In its simplest terms they suggested looking at what we do right and building on that, rather than trying to find and fix problems.

You can use it every day by changing "and" for "but" in your conversation and making meetings where every idea is a good idea and people can only build on each other's suggestions. It's easier and more useful than you think.

♒

The global pandemic had only just been declared officially, on the 5th of May 2023, but in reality, it had been gone for some time. This was a good thing. No doubt. But the implications and fall-out of Covid-19 would be with us for many more decades to come. People still complained of poor memory, and an inability to remember what had happened and when. That's not to mention the people with Long Covid. Perhaps one day in the distant future a report, film or book will pull it all together and make sense of it, like historians have a great knack for doing. Only then will we be able to evaluate and synchronise our shared experiences. One day it will all make sense to us. We'll talk about it as if we knew at the time what it meant.

For Christopher H. Bexley the adjustment was proving hard. He'd worked from home before it was fashionable, but he'd had a pandemic like few other people. What had started with him dialling into the wrong call had concluded with guns, drones and Knight of the Realm dying uncomfortably on the other side of the world. Bexley had had a busy pandemic.

Chris had had some adjusting to do.

In fairness to him, a lot had happened at a time when there was no one to talk to about it. The pubs were closed, sports was a solitary pursuit, and no one was having dinner parties. He had had a traumatic experience when everyone was looking away.

Since that time many more things in his life had changed too. Big things.

His last child, a daughter named Fleur, who he was temperamentally aligned to, had been the last to leave the little mews house in Knightsbridge. She was followed relatively quickly afterwards by her mother, and Bexley's wife, Helene. Helene was always more of a partygoer to Bex's librarian. She had gone back to the French countryside for a family reunion and promptly fell in love with a second cousin. It was awkward to say the least, but Bexley wasn't all that surprised. Plus, he reasoned, it would make Christmas easier for her family. She now had full possession of their apartment in the 6ème arrondissement in Paris. Chris had been able to keep the London house.

With Helene and Fleur gone, the house had a bit of an echo. Chris found that if he put something down somewhere it was likely to still be there when he went back. When that thing was a mug or an old sock, he had to face facts that two people do make for half as much work in running a house. He was a renaissance man. We're not talking a *Men Behaving Badly* situation here, but it wasn't easy. He ate less and cooked less and spent more time enjoying the wine cellar. It turns out that Nespresso is as good as the Italian coffee machine. Or so he felt.

All that said he was not immune from loneliness. The 'remote' nature of his work was an asset during Covid, but now he wasn't so sure. He had had a social life beforehand, playing tennis on Mondays with the 'old men' and meeting some old colleagues and classmates occasionally for drinks. But life now was different. Single people don't get invited out as often. Not to even-numbered dinner parties anyway. They don't add up. Invite another man and the dynamics are off. Invite a single women and there was an assumption. So he was discovering more of London. More of his home city. He was learning how quiet it can be, even amidst the traffic, the airplanes and the everyday blast of big city life. He enjoyed walking around the city into corners that he'd only rushed past before. He stopped and read plaques that he'd not noticed before. He sat in parks and looked curiously at the other loners sitting on distant walls and benches.

There was a rhythm to his solitude. He found ways to live in his own tunnels of routine and ritual, so that the world around fell away, and he was alone amid the over eight million people in the Capital. He found comfort in that. Joy even.

Nonetheless, Bexley was constantly having to remind himself to go sit in one of the unused bedrooms or open the door to the garage from time to time, so that dust and stale air didn't colonise the place. Already he'd had to chase a few avocados out of the house with a wooden spoon.

But he could cook, and he did. He talked on the phone all day to clients and saw them in two-dimensions, their living space, if not blurred out, was a curiosity that his mind would wander around while they talked. "Is that a guitar?" he'd think. "What lies behind the door on the left. Does she ever wear that coat on the wall? Is that a pottery, or some kind of medical equipment, in the background?" And he swam. He liked to swim.

Fundamentally though, Chris had had to admit to himself that he didn't really like people that much. Which was not something he'd ever really worried about. He was, after all, in a people business, guiding CEOs of major corporations through their weekly bouts of anxiety and allowing them to blow off some steam in their 50-minute calls. This had been his job for a long time. Pretty much his whole life, and he was okay with it, as well as being good at it.

He wasn't a 'coach'. He wasn't accredited by any of the increasingly popular, for-profit, 'coaching' organisations that offer certification for money. And he didn't like the word *coach* either. What Chris did was ask his clients to bring a list of issues to their weekly call and they worked through them together. Chris rarely offered advice, but he was very skilful at helping people to navigate their own way through the forests that had been planted by them in the first place. "So, what's going on in your world?" was often how he opened up. After each call he put in time to reload on croissants and coffee, and to write some notes.

Today was going to be a busy day. Chris raised himself up and followed his morning routine without much enthusiasm.

A little more than 50 years earlier, Arnold Jamieson Johnston had been in China. 'Jamie' to those that knew him, Johnston was a Canadian who now might be strangely recognisable because of his role in setting up the CBC and, more likely, his chancellorship of Queen's University, where a few buildings are still named after him.

Jamie cut a dapper figure wherever he went. He had a good line in tailoring without being flashy. Most of his suits seemed a size or two too large, but he wore them well. His carefully parted grey-blonde hair, his square face and easy smile, made you want to talk to him and want to please him. It was a poorly kept secret amongst his friends that Johnston has helped set up the Canadian secret service too, now known as CSIS. He'd worked in a fledgling 'propaganda' department during the second world war. His knowledge of seven languages had been a help. He'd been an itinerant soul between the wars, travelling around Europe, often on foot, and picking up languages as he went.

However, neither Mandarin nor Cantonese were languages that he spoke or understood. He'd brought a batman who did, but also in the 1970s most senior Chinese officials that he came across spoke English, sometime with a Filipino, Geordie or New Jersey accent. A few even asked him about their relatives who had long ago left for British Columbia and established businesses in small Canadian towns. Jamie always gave them time and he spoke to them all.

He'd not expected a ceremony when she arrived. He was, after all. in Chengdu, well into the interior of the country. Signs of the recent revolution were still plenty, and the standard of living was below even what Jamie had seen on his many tours of Africa. However, the bosses had somehow managed to find a bagpiper and the Canadian business envoy was now being serenaded with a choked version of Mull of Kintyre. As far as Jamie knew he had no Scottish roots, but Canada, I guess, with its long history of Scottish emigration, and its tendency to say 'out' and 'about' like a proper Glaswegian, was close enough to Scotland for the piper to be found and presented with big smiles.

Jamie was there at the invitation of the Chinese government, a senior official hailed from the region and was known to bestow random grand gestures on his people, like the visit of this quiet man from the other side of the world.

The Chinese did have work for Jamie though. They wanted to talk about mining. Canada was seen as some distance ahead of China in its mining programmes. Secretly the Chinese also admired how Canadians had been able to create an economy around natural resources, and the plundering of Earth's riches, while still being recognised for doing other, less grubby things. After Jamie had been asked to inspect the dishevelled 'guard', he was escorted to a smaller out-building where a meal was being cooked over an open fire. Chengdu is in the province of Sichuan, so Jamie knew the food would be good. Today we know it better misspelt as Szechuan.

As Jamie took off his shoes at the door and took his place on the mat, he was pleased to see young Liang Boa sit down beside him. Liang was almost young enough to be Jamie's grandchild, but the two men seemed to get along well. Jamie was both surprised and relieved to see him there. The younger man's English was excellent, and his presence meant that they were going to get to the reason why Jamie had been invited soon.

"Jamie, I am very happy you could come."

"Bao, it is always nice to see you. And I am pleased to be here. What a lovely country you have."

"Do you think?" Bao replied with a raised eyebrow.

"I do."

"How was your trip out?"

"It was uneventful, thank you."

"Was it comfortable Jamie?" Bao said sceptically.

"No, Bao, I wouldn't call it that." Jamie smiled coyly. "But I hadn't expected to be carried here on the shoulders of a cheering crowd."

"The Chinese people are always happy to make sacrifices for the nation," Bao said, not for the first time.

Jamie laughed.

The two men talked about mining, machinery and skills. Jamie knew how many Canadians were working in China. The work of the great Canadian thoracic surgeon Norman Bethune cast a long shadow in China. More than a few acolytes had followed. Jamie and Bao also talked about safety and environmental issues, although not always in those terms.

Jamie was asked what the Soviets were thinking about Finland, where skills and equipment were seen with envy by the Politburo. Boa countered with answers to Jamie's questions about Hong Kong and Macau... and Taiwan.

Bao spoke of iron ore and the amazing future he saw for it. Jamie was more interested in nickel and copper.

"What about plastic, Bao? How does the country feel about plastic? It is the future, some   say."

"'Plastics, Benjamin,' "Boa said, referencing *The Graduate* and showing that he was up to date on American culture. "I don't see it, Jamie, he said returning to the question. "Not myself. Why would you use energy to create something that you then throw away? That doesn't make sense to me." Bao straightened his linen suit. It seemed to be a size or two too big.

"Are we talking tons or tonnes?" asked Justine.

Christopher Bexley could tell already that he didn't want to talk about this. "Does it matter?" he asked, trying not to have an edge in his voice.

"Well, 204 pounds isn't negligible in the mining business, Chris. That could be the difference between profit and loss."

"Okay, but we're talking about your mines here, Justine. I was just interested to get a rough idea of output. I'm not looking to buy anything."

"Well," she laughed, "we have a good deal on iron ore this week. They're bringing up too much in the Pilbara at the moment." Chris could see the mining CEO reach back from the screen on her desk and grab a big piece of stone off a side table. "This is a hefty chunk of mineral, Chris. I am sure you could put it to some use..."

"I have quite a few doorstops already. Mostly old computers. But we're getting off topic." This was something Justine liked to do, Bexley reminded himself. "You said you wanted to talk about Mount

Marion, and the cost of production. Why is that an issue?"

"It's volatile to mine there."

"Tell me more?

"It costs a lot. There are many, many safety and security protocols. How you store the product is important. You have to keep a giant perimeter around the mine, because of the threats of outside actors."

"But that's just the cost of doing business, isn't it?" Bex had always had mining clients and so he knew a bit about the industry, probably only enough to make himself sound stupid, but he persisted.

"Well, it is for us. But not for so many others. And that is problematic."

"Are you saying you have an ethical issue?"

"No Chris, it's a business issue." She was getting impatient. "It's about how we can make this part of our business profitable. Or even *if* we can." She paused and sighed, perhaps catching herself, as CEOs so often are able to do. "It just happens to have some ethical elements."

Bexley just left the silence .

Eventually she went on.

"The other guys in places like India and China, they don't have to invest in the HSE stuff that we do. In the DRC they don't do anything. It's troubling." Chris thought to himself: that's Health, Safety and Environment, and the Democratic Republic of Congo.

"It sounds like it. Tell me more?"

"In the DRC they just let the guys – and the children – live in the mines..."

Bexley counted to 10 in his mind. She started again at seven.

"Of course, they don't live for long. But they produce stuff faster and at less cost. How can I compete with that?!

"How can you compete with that?"

"I can't!"

"Do you want to?"

"Do I want to sell more tonnage? Metric tonnes and good old fashioned regular tons! Yes, of course... We've got these accreditations. You get to differentiate between people like us who try not to kill too many people in the process – we keep the minerals stable and safe – and those who don't, and perhaps never intend to."

"So, what do you want to do?"

"...What's... right?"

Bexley laughed. "I assume so, yes."

"Fair enough. But man, ethics suck."

"Justine, we have to stop there I am sorry to say." Bexley could see he'd have to write up his notes after his next call. He was into his overlap time. But he was a creature of habit:

"Before we go, Justine, anything on your mind that we didn't cover...?"

"I am thinking of getting rid of my husband...?"

"We can cover this next time," he said with mild frustration showing in his voice. "Again."

"No, I can't think of anything. Oh, I have a meeting in Helsinki that overlaps with our next session."

"I'll speak to your assistant?"

"Yes, Chris, thanks. See if you can get me out of the meeting in Finland, can you?"

"That's not my job...."

♒

It was an hour before Bexley got to his notes. In between he'd been talking to an HR Director about a series of awkward lay-offs, driven by thinning profits. Fewer people would have to do more work, they had decided. Chris tried to keep his questioning positive and build on the good he could find.

Finally, he opened his notes file on the Mining CEO.

Justine. Business versus ESG issues. Slightly distracted. Family troubles persist. Ambitious but cautious. Issues with western requirements versus competitive practices in less regulated environments. What is worth that cost? A – Double check on next session. (He wrote in red.) Ask about succession and delegation.

Bexley's phone rattled. A BBC News story. "BREAKING: Four storey car park in Finland collapses. At least one dead. Video shows aftermath. Eastern suburb covered in dust as cloud hangs in the air. More to follow."

He consoled himself that Justine wasn't there yet... and probably didn't use multi-storey car parks anyway.

Chapter 1 – The Call

The Karpman Drama Triangle

Stephen B. Karpman was a member of the Screen Actors Guild and an extra in many movies. He was in Stephen Spielberg's first film. He was also in Harold and Maude. *Although he claimed that his Drama Triangle comes from his work in analysing American Football – it was one of six professional sports he was pleased to have competed in.*

The Drama Triangle is influenced by the Transactional Analysis *work of the Canadian Eric Berne. Berne broke with Freud by suggesting that the way in which people interacted can be seen as the ultimate guide to character. Karpman worked with Berne in California. And awkwardly it is probably Karpman's Drama Triangle that remains the more known of the two men's work.*

The Drama Triangle holds that there are three primary roles that people will play in an interaction that contains or can represent conflict. There is the Victim, the Perpetrator and the Rescuer. Each is a role, he asserts. He believed that the framework allows you to understand the roles people play and how they can move from one to another in any situation.

Bexley figured he had just enough time to get to the Wandsworth Tip before he met his psychotherapist. The Wandsworth Tip is a favourite of dads everywhere in West London. You have to book online, but then you can drive in with your car full of old rubbish and carefully mete it out into various skips. The skips have been carefully placed under a stage with great colourful labels above each: Cardboard, Large Electronics, Plants and Cuttings, etc. There were separate metal containers for things like shoes, old clothes, batteries and CDs. These big metal boxes had one-way drawers.

There was everything to like about the Wandsworth Tip. Chris was dropping off a collection of things that he'd taken down or placed in boxes, since Helene had left. He was feeling harried. Having a Tobey Jug and a clock radio and some old trainers in one box made him have to run up and down between the skips. It was a weekday so there wasn't much competition, but intuitively one always felt that the Tip was a place to show your organisational capabilities – and your muscle – to other local middle-aged men. He was failing, he felt. Tossing old shoes awkwardly into a skip filled with carpets.

He picked up the pace. Throwing things more vigorously into the bins than perhaps was necessary. He paused at the small appliances crate, where he was about to put Helene's broken alarm clock. There was a fellow there with a pole and hook that looked like something a deep-sea fisherman might use it. He was fishing old cameras, video recorders and laptops out of the tip. He quickly and casually unhooked their batteries and threw them back in. Bex was used to seeing mudlarks looking for treasure on the banks of the Thames, when the tide went out, but this seemed like a new kind of scavenger. Something very 21st century.

He was due to meet his new psychotherapist shortly and he didn't want to be late. He still had to get further into Putney and park and everything. It wasn't his first session with Andrea Spino. It also wasn't Chris's first attempt at psychotherapy. He and Helene had tried in the past, but it was clear that marriage counselling wasn't going to work for them. One or the other of them felt the counsellor was taking sides. The sessions ended before they got going.

Andrea Spino was different, Bexley thought. And this was going to be useful. He even had a short list of things he wanted to talk about. Spino kept offering to do the sessions over Skype, or Teams, or Zoom, but Bex wanted to be there, face to face. He recognised that this was somewhat hypocritical of him. He avoided actual face-to-face with people in his own practice, but he reasoned that the CEOs he dealt with weren't all as short a drive as Putney.

He skipped up the steps to the banquette where he waited. Spino was in shared rooms above a bike shop. The waiting area was just a landing and smelled like pee. The loo was a short walk up some other stairs. Presently there was a noise and Andrea appeared from the loo offering warm salutations and inviting Bex into the chamber. There were two low chairs. No sofa in sight. And a low table below the window with tissue boxes on it. Chris had never had to use those. "They get a lot of use," Andrea had said when he inquired on his first day.

In spite of the fact that Andrea was clearly of Italian extraction, and much more comfortable with emotion, Chris felt that they got along well. Andrea seemed to enjoy trying to pry the lid off Chris' reserve. So far only an occasional strip of light had been allowed in.

"How are you doing Christopher?"

"I am good thanks, Andrea. I have brought my list again. I hope you are proud of me." He opened up a notebook and propped it in the side table so they could both see it.

"Good, yes. I like a man who comes prepared. Thank you. Shall we just start with a quick centring exercise? Great. Thanks... Let's just start by closing our eyes. Find a comfortable position in the chair. Loosen your arms and legs. Let your shoulders drop. Breathe in slowly. And... then... breathe all the way out... And... one more time... in... and... out. Try to focus on your breath. Try to find a bit of compassion for yourself... Great. Thanks."

Chris always found that this part caught him off guard. But by the time he finished he felt like a different man: smaller and more compact. But also, more poised and connected. It made him wonder if he should try to learn to meditate one day.

When he opened his eyes, Andrea was there with a big, warm smile. Andrea breathed deeply one more time. He looked sideways at his notes in a plastic wallet that he had clearly written up after the discussion last time and raised a hand like an orchestra conductor.

"Just before we get going, one of the things you said last time was that you felt you weren't in good enough physical shape? We talked about setting diary times to just do some exercise 2-3 times a week? How is that going?"

"Ah, okay, well. I can report that I have put the dates in my diary. That part is working I know that."

"Ha! Okay. I get the picture."

"I'm going to keep it all though, as I think it does prompt me to do more exercise. This is really *user error*. The idea is still a good one. I will focus on it more now that some other things have settled a bit."

"Right, is that something new from this week's list? We have: *Being 'Unmarried'*; *Drinking less*; and *Impact on others* on the list. Let's start at the beginning. Tell me what you mean? Is Being Unmarried an indication that things have settled a bit?"

"I think so..."

The conversation went on for another 45 minutes while Chris discussed his marriage, the impact of the changes on his kids, concerns that he was clearing out stuff too aggressively, and worries that the neighbours saw him sneaking wine bottles into their garbage bins.

Andrea picked through it all and prompted Chris into areas where he may have been heading of his own accord.

Occasionally Andrea would put his hand on his chest and say things like "Wow, that hit me right here. That's powerful stuff. How does that feel?" And Chris would feel like he'd made progress and leave the room at the end of the session a bit lighter. He would never have really pursued it if he hadn't read a compelling article called: *The 8 Reasons Why You Shouldn't Do Therapy*. It made him feel silly for holding out. But it also made him realise the difference between what he did and what a psychotherapist did. Chris was not a psychotherapist, and he knew even better now where and how clearly to draw those lines. He also was now known to suggest some of his clients find a psychotherapist, if he felt they needed it.

♒

That night Chris made what he believes was a sophomore error. He went out for dinner with his childhood friend Tristan. They'd met on the first week of his Yorkshire prep school. It was boarding and they were eight years old. Both abandoned by their parents in a place that only had cold showers, beds with squeaky springs, and a 'nurse' who told you to take an aspirin whether you had a splinter, or you'd been knocked out in rugby practice. Chris tended to have the splinter, and Tristan the concussion. They'd been on the same rugby team, but whereas Tristan's specialty was flattening the opposition, with or without the ball, Chris' MO was to avoid all human contact.

Bexley was still built like a whippet. 5' 8" or so. About 150lbs, he had a halo of black hair that seemed to always stay that way and never give way to baldness, even though there wasn't much hair there. He had high cheekbones and deep-set eyes that looked at once sad and clever.

Tristan was none of that. His hands were like big, fleshy cushions. These days the upholstery was a bit rough, but there was still a hugeness about him, and a softness. Put a baseball hat on Tristan and he probably looked like any other middle-aged man on a golf course. He was tall but gravity had pulled his weight to the centre of his fame, and he'd stubbornly refused to buy too many new suits, shirts or trousers. His shirt-buttons looked like they could take an eye out at any moment. His suits got rumpled by him simply putting them on.

But Tristan worked in finance and that meant that he'd been able to channel his charm into accounts, commissions, and sales for the Bank of Chicago's Corporate Bank. These days his accent could modulate like radio trying to find a station. He was inclined to start and end sentences with the word *mate*, in a way that would have been prohibited by his headmaster and his mother, in that order.

"Bex... what are we doing? We are going to end up old and alone, with no one to empty our colostomy bags. Mate, we're a bit fucked, aren't we!"

Tristan had heard that Bex was now flying solo, and he thought that was reason enough to go out to a nice restaurant and order a few bottles of wine.

"Tris, I am fine. Not sure about you, but I am fine. I have a full schedule and the kids sometimes see me. I am good."

Tristan looked at him for a while. He pushed his chair out further and moved his legs out from under the table. He pulled a vape from his pocket and put it in his moth without exhaling any smoke.

"Is that right, mate? Tell me, what did you do last night?"

Chris looked a bit nervous, then annoyed. "I was... busy. It was a busy day. I worked until about 8, then made some dinner and went to bed. Why?"

"And what about the night before?"

"Um. Um. Tristan, what are you trying to say?"

"What do you think?"

"That I am boring?"

"No! We're all boring! This bloody pandemic has taken all the fun out of our lives." He was waving his arms around dramatically, drawing attention to the table. Bexley cringed a bit, inside. "...And we're intent on sitting at home and doing nothing like we did for the better part of two years. The theatres are empty, the pubs are turning into condos, when we used to worry that the banks were turning into wine bars. We're a nation... a world... of shut-ins."

"I agree there is some readjusting to do..."

"When did you last go away?"

"Well, I did that thing during Covid that got me in the papers a bit. That was a lot of travel."

"That sounded more like a hostage situation to me, matey. I'm talking about going somewhere for no reason?"

"I'm not interested in shooting, Tris. And I don't enjoy golf. I get out. I have run. Recently."

"I know. I know. I'm not saying you are not trying or that you are boring. Promise. I wonder though, how do we... well, here I am really talking about *me*... how do I become actually *interesting*?"

"What do you mean?"

"I wonder mate, are we taking advantage of what the world has to offer? I want to be *interesting*. I want to have hobbies and things to say. I want to talk to people about things that don't involve financial instruments, alimony, or ... bloody school fees."

Dinner was fine. Chris tried not to think about Tristan as a client. He didn't want to imagine him sliding around Karpman's Drama Triangle. But he couldn't stop himself. Victim, Ding! Rescuer. Ding-ding! Perpetrator. Perpetrator. Perpetrator. Ding, ding, ding.

Tristan wasn't alone. Along with seeing the psychotherapist Andrae Spino, Bexley had been doing his own research into psychology and mental health. It was an area that was adjacent to his skills, but he'd never really given it enough attention. He'd taken a psychology elective in university, but that seemed to involve too much biology. Bex wasn't that interested then.

Now, however, he reasoned that the work of Doctors Freud and Jung were more than 100 years old, there must be something to them. They were older than penicillin and nuclear war. Something had made them durable.

In talking to people like Tristan Hope-Hartley Chris was inclined to think about what Carl Jung, the dour Swiss-German had had to say about 'anima'. That we are all chasing our real-selves. That as we get older we are trying to reconcile ourselves to who we really are, rather than the 'playing grown-ups' that we have been doing most of our lives. The Anima, Jung says, was like a shadow that we are trying to fit into.

"What do you enjoy doing Tris?" Bex asked him.

"What do you mean? I mean, golf, long lunches, and making money… Is that what you mean?"

"No." Bex replied. He was trying to stop himself from coming across as a bored school teacher.

"I like shooting. I like skiing in the Alps, or in the Rockies. Like that?"

"I'm not sure," said Bexley. "What I am getting at is, if you had a week off and no obligations. If no one cared or noticed what you did, what would you do?"

"Well, I don't know," Hope-Hartley looked thoughtful and suspicious at the same time. "Is it important?"

"It may be important to finding out what would make you interesting."

"What if I really don't know...?" Tristan wasn't having this.

"Well, we've known each other for a long time, so let me point at a few things for you." Bexley said, as Hope-Hartley ordered another bottle of wine. "You used to do a lot of theatre at school. You used to read a lot of science fiction. You organised an touch rugby team at university..."

"Ha! Imagine all 17 stone of me running around chasing a frisbee!"

"What are you passionate about? And don't say wine..."

"Well, it's true."

"Yes, but it's not a hobby. It's not interesting to anyone. It's more like a slow suicide note than an interesting pastime. You need to think what you are curious about. What gives you a slight spring in your step? What do you want to know more about? What posters in the Tube make you raise an eyebrow...?"

By the end of the evening Bexley was more tired than he'd have liked to have been. But he was also quite drunk, so he went home and had a glass of Port and a cheese sandwich and went to bed.

The phone rang early, early the next morning. Chris opened one eye at a time. He was good at switching off his mobile. Even after an evening of trying to be interesting and drinking expensive wine.

It was his landline. That number wasn't something that was easy for people to find any more. The only one who ever called on it was Helene's uncle… Chris' soon-to-be ex-uncle-in-law.

Chris slowly did the calculation in his head and found that the idea that Helene might be unwell made him jump. He got to the phone on the fourth ring and answered like a man who'd seen a fire.

"Pierre ?! Qu'est-ce qui ce passe ?"

But it wasn't Pierre. A quiet woman's voice spoke hesitantly. "Christopher? I am SO sorry. It's early there…"

"What? Who is this?" Chris reached for his head unconsciously.

"It's Justine. Justine Jurys. I have a problem."

It took Bexley what seemed like a long time to connect the speaker with a person he knew and longer still for him to understand that she didn't sound right.

Justine was in Philadelphia. Not somewhere she went to often. But she'd been told to meet an important contact there. She was booked into the Four Seasons on Benjamin Franklin Parkway. The broad avenue in central Philadelphia, is most well-known for the Rocky films, in which Sylvester Stallone runs down the parkway and jumps up and down in front of the art museum. It is a beautiful American avenue in the spirit of Commonwealth Avenue in Boston and The Mall in DC. He was going to send a car or find her at about 10 am. Justine had woken early and done some emails. She'd had a call with her team in Singapore about a deal. Then she had casually gone down to the breakfast buffet at the hotel restaurant. But when she got back to her seat with a plate of fruit and scrambled eggs, there was a note at her chair. She looked around and then sat down and read it.

"Make Li low", it said in an awkward script.

Justine looked around again. No one seemed out of place. No sudden movements.

She put her napkin onto the table and got up again. She went to find the person at the entry to the breakfast room. No one was there. She went back into the breakfast room. Her table was clear, her purse and phone were gone. No one was sitting close enough to ask. The staff weren't around. She walked out to reception and up to the Concierge.

"Can you help? I am not sure what just happened. I think I have been robbed?"

"Oh dear, Madam, that's not good. Are you staying with us? What is your name?" The Concierge hovered over the keyboard.

"Jurys. Justine Jurys. Jay-Ewe-Arr-Why-Ess." She was distracted and looking around for someone carrying her things. Confused.

"I am afraid we don't have anyone staying here under that name. Did you come in with someone?" Justine could see the Concierge looking over her shoulder for hotel security. Justine reached into her trouser pocket and felt the card-key for her room. She looked up and smiled pleasantly.

"That will be fine. Thank you." And she turned and walked to the elevator. One opened immediately and she got in. She took it to the 4th floor. Opening her room door, she saw the bed was made and all her belongings were gone. She checked the number on the door again. It was the right door. She closed it quickly and put the deadbolt on. She went to the door to the adjoining room and checked that that was securely closed too.

She sat on the bed and pressed the Operator button on the hotel room phone. "Can you get me international directory assistance please?"

"It's Justine. Chris, I need help." Bexley heard her say again. She was composed, but not her confident self.

"What's happening Justine? What can I do?"

"I'm not sure. I'm in the U.S. and something is happening. Sorry to call you, but you were on my mind. I'm here to talk about a new mine in Australia. There's interest from some countries we don't normally talk to."

"Are you in trouble?"

"I think I may be. But I'm not sure how much. Have you heard of a guy called Lang? Bob Lang?"

"No. I don't think so. But you know I don't get out much." He wrote down the man's name.

"I was meant to go... wait... Sorry Chris. I have to go." And with that the line went dead. He punched in her name and called her mobile. It came up as unknown. He tried her on video-conference. Nothing.

Bexley didn't know what to do. He jumped up and went downstairs. Then he came upstairs again. He got a glass of water. He put some clothes on. Then he sat down and made some notes.

He looked through a notebook from 2022. May…he was looking for. He found the number. He dialled.

“Hello?”

“Brett? Have I woken you up? I am very sorry it’s Christopher Bexley… I work with Justine…”

“Chris. Yes. I am asleep. Let me just turn on a light…”

There was whispering. Brett could be heard reassuring someone.

“I am awake. Are you okay? What can I do? Why are you calling?”

“I am really sorry. I am fine. But I am worried about Justine. I have just hung up with her…”

“Oh, Chris, you’re not getting wrapped up in this are you? She’s sent me papers. The marriage is being annulled… I can’t…”

“No Brett, it’s not about that. It’s her safety.” There was a pause. “Do you know where she is? She’s in the U.S., in Philadelphia. She called to say she was in trouble and the line went dead. I think she may be in physical distress…”

“Christ,” Brett said quietly. “When was this? Did she say what hotel she was at?”

“She is at the Four Seasons in the centre of town.” Chris said, again consulting his notes.

“Let me call the company’s head of Security. He’s a decent guy. And ex-Marine. Can you fire up your computer? I’ll get him on a video call with us…”

"Yes. Thanks Brett. That would be good. I'll be here."

It was almost an hour before they were on screen together again. The Security guy was in the office. Brett was in a dark room. Chris had made himself some coffee. Talking to Justine had rattled him and he was struggling to settle. The video call was blessedly short. There was no sign of Justine that the company could now find. They had involved local police and the staff was being interviewed one by one. This, in itself, was already a lot of work. No one is really a Missing Person until they have been gone for more time than Justine. However, her firm can be quite persuasive, and the local police were interested in what had happened. No one likes for a CEO to go missing on their watch.

Chris had to relay his story again. The questions he faced focused on two areas: Who was she meeting (Chris didn't know; why would he?) and then "Bob Lang". Who was Bob Lang?

Bexley didn't have a clue, of course. There were literally thousands of them on LinkedIn.

Chris managed to ask about the "countries we don't normally do business with" and the new mine, but he didn't get an answer. There was less interest in that part of the story.

When the call was over, Chris was restless. He dug deep into his chest of drawers and the back of the suddenly quite empty closet... and he pulled out his running kit. He stretched awkwardly, possibly pulling a muscle in his groin, and headed out towards Hyde Park.

Chapter 2 – The Escape

The Transition Curve

True to form for psychologists of the day, Elisabeth Kübler-Ross was Swiss-German. She was born in Zurich in 1926 and had an eventful childhood. She was one of triplets, weighing just two pounds at birth. This frailty was likely the reason she contracted pneumonia at age five. While hospitalised she experienced the peaceful death of the girl in the bed next to her. By age 13 she was a lab assistant in World War II. She left home at 16 and did relief work in seven of the larger European countries after the war. She was a self-funded doctor by the age of 31 and a psychiatrist six years later. Her book "On Death and Dying" in 1969, gave us the 'five stages of grief' that have been handily abused since. Kübler-Ross had no 'curve' and simply referred to Denial, Anger, Bargaining, Depression and Acceptance as the five stages one goes through when facing death – one's own or someone else's. She had no interest in business (refusing her father's entreaties to take a secretarial role in his firm) and would likely not have recognised the term Change Management. Yet she is cited today in business courses around the world as the source of The Change Curve.

"Jussi, how are you, dude? Did your band play last night?" Lulu stopped to ask as she crossed the floor of the Huhta-Pak factory in Helsinki. She was on her way to the office, but tried to walk through the production area when she did. Some of her colleagues weren't interested in the production of plastics, or the people who operated the vats and machines that punched out the sheets, boxes and packaging that Huhta-Pak created every day.

Lulu wasn't one of these people. Although she worked in Commercial, she was a scientist by training. She had a Biophysical Chemistry degree from McGill University in Canada. She knew what was going on on the floor and appreciated the people who made the products.

"The band didn't play, Lulu. But we have a gig on Friday night at the MadHatter in town. Will you come watch?"

"I'd like to. Let me see what I can do."

Although Lulu hadn't been in Finland for very long. She liked the place. The people here had a Nordic spirit that she recognised from home. The aggressors in bars and clubs here were the women, not the men. A good-looking bloke would get drinks sent to him all night in town. And women appearing at his elbow to offer them. That seemed like a nice change to Lulu.

She could get self-conscious about the fact that her Finnish was rudimentary at best. German didn't help her. French, Spanish and Italian were irrelevant. The closest European language to Finnish was

Hungarian… and that was not one of the languages that Lulu had mastered.

She had been in the capital city for almost 10 months now. She had swum in the harbour at 6 am. They had cut a meter-wide hole cut in the ice to get into the frigid water of the harbour. Her apartment had a sauna in it. It was accessed via a ladder that pulled down in front of the entry to her kitchen. It was built into the eaves of the wooden building. She'd embraced the practice. Her pores were now the size of pennies.

She had also embraced the so-called Scandi-noir detective novel. She had read Stig Larsson before she arrived in the Baltics, but she was able to make quick work of the dozens of novels by Henning Mankell. She'd tried Jo Nesbo, but found it too graphic. Peter Høeg, Arnaldur Indriðason, Jussi Adler-Olsen and Camilla Läckberg were filling out her book shelves now. She always had a book in hand when she arrived at work, and usually displayed it on her desk. This invited discussions and also showed she was paying attention to her surroundings. Or so she hoped.

Recently she'd had one of her rare moments of fear in Scandinavia. A car park had collapsed near the centre of town. The Finns had been amongst the fastest adopters of Electric Vehicles, or EVs. However, the world isn't completely ready yet for EVs. The new cars generally weigh almost twice as much as their combustion-engine cousins. An old car park in central Helsinki had given way under the weight.

She could see smoke and dust over the city for 48 hours.

Lulu was here at Huhta-Pak to work on a new and untested chemical particle. Holstium wasn't known to her before she arrived. "I never read that far in the Periodic Table," she had said in her interview. After all her time in Helsinki, she still wasn't entirely sure about it.

She understood the theory. Holstium could be used to create a lighter, less volatile, plastic that could be used to store energy in batteries. It was cheaper, easier and a potential major jump forward in the whole transition away from fossil fuels.

The speed at which all of these things were happening, and the interest and competition meant that Lulu's work here was very much on the bleeding edge of science and commerce. Her task so far had been to help explain what the new material could do and get more funding to help develop it faster.

The bit that she was much less clear about was whether it worked… or even existed.

She was very good and practiced at asking questions without raising concerns or interest. But the answers weren't particularly forthcoming. It wasn't clear where the project was being run from, or even who was in control of it. She and her colleagues had received instruction from each other, but it was hard to trace it all back to a single source.

One thing that was very clear to her however was that the efforts so far to create a single, common product had been hampered by a regular and unsettling set-back. Holstium wasn't stable it all. In fact, it was very volatile. When the fire engines came to a factory like Huhta-Pak, the senior managers could usually talk their way out of too much suspicion. They could do this easily once. The second time was trickier. It wasn't fully clear what number call-out they were on now, but it was more than three and less than a dozen. Lulu had been there for four in the last 10 months.

There wasn't ever anything too scary. No one lost an arm or an eye. That would have brought a very different kind of attention. But there were some very bright flames, a few pops that couldn't be ignored, and the fire alarms in this part of the world were sensitive. Fire likes cold air. One time the building had been evacuated for a strong odour that Lulu suspects she'll never really get cleared out of her nostrils.

The upside, of course, was the actual firemen. In Finland they weren't self-conscious or vain in the way that too many Firemen of The Year calendars had made them back home. But they were fine, she was comfortable saying.

They arrived with bells ringing and dressed warmly even in a Finnish winter. But as they assessed the situation and got more accustomed to walking around the plant and the offices the kit was undone and hanging around them as they walked. It wasn't an unpleasant result. Even if the events that were less desirable. Lulu had even become quite Finnish briefly and pressed her details into the big hand of one particular green-eyes wonder.

Unfortunately, no bells had rung after that.

It is possible that Lulu was daydreaming when the phone buzzed on her desk. She turned it over. The sender of the new WhatsApp message was listed as "1941 Ogilvie" and it said: "Unload. Come in."

She sighed. "Oh man. Really? Dudes. What the fuck?" All that perhaps a bit louder than she had meant to. When she looked up the colleagues nearest to her were looking at her. She blushed a bit.

"Sorry," she said. "I gotta go. There's something wrong at home." She gathered up her book and phone, but not much else and headed out of the offices, down the stairs and across the floor. Outside the plant her bright white SUV, rented when she arrived, was parked in the Executive Parking. That meant she was close to the exit and out onto the highways near Espoo... and gone.

♒

Christopher Bexley wasn't an ugly man. Not least for a man of his age. He looked thoughtful and intelligent. The cut of the clothes, and attention to grooming, was too good to be casual, but equally wasn't fussy. He could blend into a crowd, but if he spoke directly with you, his easy smile and the way he held your gaze made an impression.

Chris was busily putting things into a leather carrying case. Too big to be a briefcase, but also small enough to be carried onto a plane without much worry.

He had already packed and re-packed once. He'd initially thought he was heading into the relative summer warmth of Pennsylvania. But developments had changed his course. He was now going to be in the air longer, crossing Europe and Asia to get to the west coast of Australia.

He wasn't entirely sure what he was doing or why. He knew that he didn't like Australia. "There's nothing there," he would grumble to close friends when the topic arose. That obviously wasn't a commonly held view for the thousands of students who went there to find themselves on a gap-year. Or for the Doctors and Nurses who could imagine themselves surfing after a shift. Although no study has yet been published of how many ever did.

Before he called a cab, he checked his watch and put in a call to Mrs Springer.

"Mrs Springer, it's Chris. Chris Bexley."

"Yes, Christopher."

"I am on my way to Australia."

"Yes. Yes, you are."

Mrs Springer had been the secretary to the recently deceased industrialist Malcolm Goddard. Springer and Goddard had not gotten along. He referred to her as the 'bloody German', even though he knew she was Austrian. She had patiently and effectively managed his life very well. Even though he wasn't often cooperative. When his life came to a sudden end, she had approached Chris about working for him. Chris had always managed his own diary and done so effectively. Mrs Springer had been able to show him quickly how wrong he was. Still, he hadn't had enough work to keep her going full time, so she took on two or three other clients as well. Bexley didn't know who they were, but he trusted her implicitly.

"I'm going to need some help."

"I can book your flights now. We'll go through Singapore. On Singapore Airways. You're going to Perth, right?"

"Yes, but I don't know how you knew that?"

"Don't worry. Mr Hatch will meet you at the airport. He has some things for you."

"*What?* I am not going with *Hatch*! How did he know about this?! Tell him to leave me alone."

"Christopher, it is not my affair what happens when you and he meet, but he assures me that he will have things that you will need…"

"And, Springer, when did he assure you of that?" He caught himself, as he was suddenly starting to sound like Malcolm Goddard. That wasn't something Bexley ever wanted to do. "I am sorry Mrs Springer. I will look for him there. Can you get me hotel room in Perth? And I may need a rental car. Can you give me information on that? Because once I am out there, it won't be a good time of day to call you when I need one."

"I will forward that on WhatsApp."

"Lovely. Thank you, Mrs Springer. I really appreciate it." He knew that his supplications were pointless with her, but he still felt badly for raising his voice.

♒

Justine was in the back of a private plane. It wasn't particularly luxurious, but it wasn't set out to be a commercial flyer either. She could tell that. There was no one around her but she could see some heads and hear some muffled voices in a clutch of seats up ahead of her. She couldn't move. She hadn't the energy, but it also looked like her hands and feet were connected to the chair by some Velcro straps. She was clearly drugged. She recognised the effects of a muscle relaxant, but she also sensed something else. It was a sort of happy medicine. She felt elated. But it was a simulated high. She knew that her heart was still beating fast, and her blood pressure was likely up. However, the feeling was still very nice. She had no idea where she was, why she was there, or what might happen next. But she was happy. There was something in that.

♒

Justine had clearly dozed again. Because she was now in a warm and comfortable room. Not quite like a home, but comfortable like a hospice or a retirement home. She wasn't alone either. She was in a bed with wires and tubes attached to her. And there were others there in a similar fix. At least two. It didn't seem crowded though and that warm feeling of happiness was still there. She was trying to take things in, to remember some of the detail, but she felt tired again and turned her face to the pillow.

♒

Lulu's mind turned to the oil-tank truck she had crossed as she left the plant in Huhta-Pak a few hours previously. She was in a lounge at Heathrow awaiting her next out-bound flight. The sound was off on the TV, but she could recognise the setting in the pictures. She didn't recognise the building, because it was largely gone. But she did recognise the landscape around it. She had worked there for almost a year. The explosion must have been a big one. She was surprised because she knew there was nothing there worth blowing up: some lunch cartons, lots of harmless people, and some failed research.

Lulu was used to strange happenings and curious wisdom behind important decisions. But this seemed like a very unsubtle and a blunt attack. She was, she recognised, quite angry.

♒

Bob Lang liked living in Philadelphia. The healthcare was good – if you had good insurance. He did. There are more MRI machines in Philadelphia than there are in all of Canada. He lived in a nice house on a quiet street in Wayne, Pennsylvania. The neighbours were kind. They didn't ask any questions. They nodded to each other in their yards. He wasn't far from the famous King of Prussia Mall. He liked to take people there who came from back home, because it was so big and, well, excessive. It was one of the biggest malls in America and had more than 450 retailers in it. But he avoided it himself. He didn't like that much open space with so many people.

Over time Lang's accent had taken on a soft Philadelphia edge to it. It could be heard when he said words like *ham*, *mayonnaise* and *Nancy*, where the letter A became more like a long E. He was proud of that. It helped him to blend in.

Lang's offices were in an office complex a short drive down the Lancaster Road, Conestoga and Valley Forge to Chesterbrook. He liked the fact that building had once been the offices of the British firm

AstraZeneca. It gave the place a bit of corporate history. Lang had always believed that the Americans needed more history. They only had a few hundred years and they milked it like mad. The made-up events to commemorate, and they created monuments that would have made the Ancient Egyptians blush. To Lang, American history was another country. Their own magical mythology machine in Los Angeles had been creating stories and legends that filled more literature than Ancient Rome and Athens combined. Modesty or restraint was not something the Americans were good at, Lang felt. And he admired that.

In spite of himself, Lang collected things. He liked to buy nice furniture. He had his house done by a local interior decorator that he had read about in the Philadelphia Life magazine. He felt that the house was understated in an East Coast way. But it also showed. It showed wealth without being gauche, as the locals would say.

Unfortunately, Bob Lang was also a bit of an impulsive buyer. His giant garage, which most Americans have at the end of a driveway, that could fit 3-4 cars. It was full, but not of cars. He wasn't proud of all the contents either. There were a lot of things that he had bought off of late-night television. A bottle cutter. An LP player, that didn't really work. Some mysterious fitness equipment. A grill that was unopened.

That wasn't all though. He was often to be found stopping at roadside "Antique" shops. He had tin signs for Lucky Strike cigarettes. A neon light saying "Open 'Til Late". And a whole carton of empty boxes for McDonald's Happy Meals... along with the requisite toys. These at least were stacked carefully. He had a ledger on his laptop saying where he'd got them, and the response he'd received.

Chapter 3 – FIFO

Hofstede's Cultural Dimensions

The Dutch academic Geert Hofstede is still the most frequently cited social scientist of all time. He died in 2020 in his 92nd year, with books published in 23 languages. However, over his long and celebrated career it could be argued he helped put his own theories and research out of business. After the second world war he travelled from his home in the Netherlands to the United Kingdom to see a girl he had met. What he found in England so shocked him that it altered the course of his life. Hofstede, who trained as a mechanical engineer, morphed into a psychologist. He studied people and cultures. He worked in leadership development at IBM. He proposed in his seminal work Cultural Dimensions *that there are six dimensions to different national cultures. "Power Distance" is one. Different levels of Individualism and Masculinity are two more. The final three are "Uncertainty Avoidance", Long-Term Orientation and "Indulgence vs Restraint". He then set about mapping nation\al cultures and discussing each. And while the books remain interesting, and fun, the increased interaction and cross-pollination of cultures has dulled some of the impact.*

Although he spent hours each day in one chair, looking at a screen, the move from his desk to an airline seat felt like a hairshirt to Bexley. He started and gave up on at least a half-dozen films. He poked at the tiny screen, but got no satisfaction. He writhed and twitched in his place like a tired infant. He had brought things to read but it felt like the white-noise of the plane was jamming his receptors. He stared at the pages without taking anything in.

It was going to be a long trip.

He blamed Johnny Heck.

John Hatch, who, for reasons unknown, Bex called Johnny Heck, was a school mate in Yorkshire and then he also knew Chris through into university. Chris knew that Hatch had gone into the military after that, but they had lost touch. Until Hatch had turned up at the Bexley's house mid-Covid. Things had become quite unpredictable since.

In fact, Bexley hadn't seen him since they had been together cleaning up a mess at the top Montreal's Mount Royal two years ago. He tried to remember if it actually was two years ago? Covid had made even that unclear.

When Bexley arrived at Heathrow airport to catch his flight to Perth, he had cleared customs, and was walking around trying to find the least expensive coffee, when Hatch had approached him. He'd quickly spirited Chris into the Virgin Atlantic lounge and they had found a quiet corner.

“Right Bex, here’s your new passport,” Hatch handed him a blue passport. Bexley looked back at him warily and opened it up. The picture was recent. The name was unfamiliar. “That’s not all, there’s this one too,” Hatch proffered a green one. Bex snorted when he saw the name of the country it came from. “There are two more in this folder, and drivers’ licences too, and a Monzo card – which operates as cash in most countries. Try to keep track of them. But do know that we’ll be able to see where you are when you use any of them… which should be reassuring.”

At that Bexley lost his temper.

He didn’t make too much noise or cause a scene, but he ranted about presumptions, and cheek; about being tired, and not having signed up for this. Hatch listened intently, without changing his expression. Bexley had quite a lot to say. After a while Hatch did look over Bexley’s shoulder at the LED display that was behind him.

Bexley finally slowed down and stopped. Hatch looked at him and stared for a minute. “You’re going to Australia, right?”

“Yes,” Bexley looked suspicious.

“Why?” Hatch asked.

“Because my friend may be in trouble, and I think that Australia may be the best place to try to find her…” Chris seemed a bit unsure.

“I think you are right,” Hatch said. “And all I want to do is help...”

"Last time that didn't end up that well, though Johnny, did it?!" Bexley spat out.

Hatch paused for roughly a 10 count. Bexley recognised the tactic.

"What happened in Montreal was a success. It might not have seemed that way, but it was."

"Tell that to my therapist," Bexley said. More quietly, sensing defeat now.

Hatch pulled out another folder. "This is more background that you'll need to read. The flight will give you time."

Bexley took it and opened the first page. "Lithium? *Lithium*. Are you having me committed? Isn't that what they gave Rose Kennedy? It's an anti-depressant, no? I've heard of Curt Cobain…"

Hatch put up his hand. Bexley stopped.

"Lithium is number 3 on the periodic table. That makes it Atomic Number 3. Its abbreviation is Li. It is the least dense metal in the world and also the lightest. But that doesn't mean it is stable. It is highly flammable and tends to need to be stored in a vacuum." Hatch looked up. "That's an airless chamber. Not a Hoover."

Bexley made a face.

"When it does come in contact with air it corrodes. It turns silver and grey and then black."

"It is also notoriously hard to mine. You can get it out of ocean water, from brines. Which has always been exciting because that means it is a renewable resource. There are estimates that there is over 200 billion tonnes of Lithium in sea water." Bexley was about to ask whether that was *tonnes* or *tons*. He stopped himself.

"Back in the day it was also a key part of a nuclear reactor. I shouldn't say 'back in the day', we are still using lots of nuclear reactors today. And it is obviously part of nuclear warheads."

"Shit," said Chris quietly.

"We also know it from Nirvana, yes. There are Lithium-based drugs that are seen as mood stabilisers. Like anti-depressants. Governments and – ah – militaries have been interested in that side of it too, for a long time. I am happy saying I don't know much about that."

"The problem is that taking Lithium from sea water is a long, slow and labour-intensive process. So, there is a preference to mine it from minerals. That is where some of the issues come in. The largest reserves in the world are in the Democratic Republic of Congo. The DRC. They have 1.5 billion tonnes, one estimate says."

Bexley interrupted. "Is that mined in tunnels? Where the miners, including children, are known to sleep in the tunnels? While mining this extremely unstable metal?"

"Yes." Hatch looked at him without blinking. "It takes almost 2 million litres of water to produce one ton of

Lithium. That water is then poisonous and can infect river water and even the water table. It causes respiratory illnesses, plant life is affected, there is magnesium and lime created in the process that need to be dealt with... To say nothing of the fact that Lithium is relatively easy to make go 'boom'. So, it is a target for terrorists, or western security agencies that want to cause trouble. There's Lithium in fireworks."

Bexley nodded. "After the DRC, where is the second largest source of Lithium?"

"Australia."

"Yes."

Hatch stood up. "Your flight is boarding." He handed Chris another envelope. "You are not boarding as Chris Bexley. Here's your new boarding card. You'd better go."

Bexley gave his friend an angry glance before leaving.

Now shuffling in his seat, Bexley was replaying all that Hatch had told him. This was going to be a long flight, he decided. He tried closing his eyes. Just then, a few seats away, someone sneezed loudly. A woman screamed in surprise. Bex swore softly under his breath. He pulled an eyeshade over his eyes.

Lulu was waiting in the plastic chairs outside the flight. The lady at the check-in was paging a Mr Christopher Bexley. No one was responding. There was a short man with dark hair, standing beside her looking around the room as the announcement was made.

Lulu went back to her briefing documentation. She was reading about the global war for Lithium. The mineral as used in many modern appliances. It was the basis for the Electric Vehicle. “And EVs are the future…”, she could hear a voice in her head saying.

The ‘war’ had to do with mining companies fighting for the right to access Lithium mines in different countries. There had already been reports out of the so-called Lithium Triangle (Chile, Argentina and Bolivia) about miners and governments cheating indigenous people out of their rights. ‘Cheating’ was the term that was argued over.

That kind of thing burnt Lulu’s bagels. She was annoyed by it.

What she didn’t know was why lithium batteries in cars made them so heavy. She did know that there were worries that we were taking on EVs too fast. Cars and even car parks were liable to more damage because of the additional weight that an EV has compared to a petrol car. And although car parks were the same size, cars were getting bigger.

Just then, the men beside Lulu sneezed, and Lulu let out an involuntary scream.

“Oh, my God. I am SO sorry,” the man said. His wife leaned over and smiled at Lulu too.

“I know,” she said. “It’s crazy, isn’t it. I keep telling him he’s exaggerating.”

“That’s just how I sneeze,” he said curtly.

“Don’t worry,” Lulu said to them, laughing. “That’s a hell of a sound though. You can’t be too popular when they’re getting the cocaine out…”

The two strangers paused, looked at her and turned away. “I’m sorry’” she said. “I have a rotten sense of humour.”

They got to talking. The couple were on their way back to Perth from London. “He hates it, I love it,” she explained. “The Brits are just too stiff,” he said. Then he looked worried. You’re not British, are you?”

Lulu shook her head, her long brown hair flying about. “Nope. I’m Canadian. From Calgary, in the west.”

“Oh, yes,” the lady jumped in, “the Olympics! And…” she paused, “another mining town.”

“Sort of. It’s an energy town, for sure. And there are cowboys and stampedes.”

“We should go there one day,” the woman said to her partner.

“What do you guys do?” Lulu asked.

“We’re FIFOs,” the man said. “That means Fly-In, Fly-Out. We live in Perth, but we work further north in the

Pilbara… that's a mining district in the north-west of Australia."

"I've heard of it," Luly said. "What's it like?"

"It's a desert basically. We live in an air-conditioned porta-cabin when we are up there. And drive around in massive, air-conditioned trucks when we are working."

"The tyres on my truck are 4 meters high," said the woman excitedly. "That's like as big as this plane is tall."

"And you are… miners?" Lulu looked sceptical. They might have been younger than her and they were wearing similar clothes. The pair both nodded. "Wow," said Lulu as she felt that was appropriate to say. "Did you both always want to be miners?"

"Ha! Are you kidding!" They both spoke rapidly.

"I used to be a teacher," the man said. "A maths teacher."

"He was good too," the lady said. "And I was a lawyer. A trademark lawyer."

"We just couldn't afford to do it anymore," he explained. "This is a significant pay rise. Working as miners. A *big* one." His wide eyes told the story.

"Wow." Lulu said again.

Kenny and Maureen were their names. They chatted away happily for a while, but it was also a long flight. Lulu managed to fit in a few films too.

The border guards in Australia are very aggressive. Only the United States of America are they more aggressive. And there might be a tie. Both are awful. Bex knew this but he was still surprised when he was questioned in rapid shots, told to "just answer the questions", and then taken into an anteroom for further discussions. In fairness to him he'd been reading an NYT article about Lithium in Australia, and he hadn't really paid that much attention. So, when he got to the counter, he wasn't prepared to answer some quite basic questions: What's your name? Why is a Belarussian coming to Australia?

He had however been reading some surprising information about the Lithium mines in Oz.

- Spodumene, a green powder that was only 6% lithium would sell at about £4,500 per ton.
- China was the key buyer for EVs, cell phones and other battery-centric uses.
- More than half of the world's Lithium comes from Australia.
- All of it gets sold to China. *All of it.*

The basic calculus was that Australia no longer wanted to export it, they wanted to create the end product with it. Batteries, cars, e-bikes. The lot. There was more margin to be made in that. More money. But also the Aussies reasoned, quite reasonably that they should make their own product that needed lithium rather than exporting the metal and buying back the products made with it.

They also would have liked to sell it to clearer allies like the USA or South Korea.

If the Australians could refine the spodumene to a lithium phosphate silt, they would already break a key step in the supply chain, where China had stolen a march. The Australian needed to decide if the AU $70 million investment was worth it. They'd already poured hundreds of millions into the industry, so it seemed a no-brainer.

The Americans were in favour. Biden's Inflation Reduction Act supported a market in Australia.

The Chinese: not so much.

But the Chinese were way, way ahead when it came to the cost of production. As someone once said, the Chinese people are always happy to make sacrifices for the nation. That translated to a 250% higher cost of production in Australia to that of China.

It may not have been fair, but it was fact.

Geopolitics wasn't Bex's strong suit. But he did feel he knew one thing for sure: If Australia had the product, and China needed it, then the Aussies had the whip-hand.

But, perhaps more immediately, the guy in the uniform with the buzz-cut had left the room with his passport. And the remaining kid was doing his best to look menacing. Processing the situation, Bex did his best impression of someone who was scared. He was pleased that he hadn't smiled. Then suddenly the original thug came back. He was beet-red.

"I am so sorry Minister Kotova. Please accept the warm welcome of the Australian government." The man with the big red head was saying the words, but his face wasn't selling it. The kid's jaw had dropped. Bexley thought he saw a bit of drool hit the table.

"Thank you... I love Australia," Bex said in his best Eastern European bad-guy accent. He wasn't doing a good job, but fortunately the two men from Australia were even less discriminating than Bex when it came to Bond-villain accents.

He gathered up his green passport and walked through customs, head held high.

When Lulu got through security in Perth, Wendy and Georgia were there to meet her. They weren't work colleagues, they were a couple that Lulu had worked with early in her career. They were both lawyers now and had two daughters who were approaching teenage years. They took Lulu to their bungalow in Victoria Park.

They had bought it when they were just starting out, but it was clear that, as the money came, so did the investment. They had a pool. The house was now mostly glass and chrome. And the kids had a parade of friends that seemed to come and go. Lulu was shown to a guest house by the pool that was modern but still had the feel of a guest house at the Chateau Marmot in Los Angeles. It had character.

Low and flat and green, Victoria Park stretched around one side of the Swan River, which had created a natural bay before rolling out into the southwest coast of Australia. There were beaches, simple water pursuits and a lovely temperate weather, year-round. It wasn't an easy city to get to, but it was an easy place to live.

She could get used to this.

When she returned to the poolside after unpacking a bit, there was a lovely sound as the rosé was opened.

"Dudes! This is awesome," she said.

Under her wide-leg capri pants and her camisole was a bikini, and she felt that it was time to introduce her ivory belly to some sunshine.

♒

Bexley was both more and less fortunate. The hotel that Mrs Springer had booked him was a modern wonder. It was at the top of a high street in Perth that has all the shops, stores and food outlets that Bex could have wanted. H went out and bought a wide-brimmed hat as a first order of business (sun had no business on his pale skin). There were no corks hanging from the brim of the hat – although those head been on offer – but it presented a nice balance between practicality and cover.

What was remarkable though was the look out of the other side of the hotel. The side that Chris' room faced onto. It was a look out to sea. Chris wasn't a cartographer, but he reckoned that if he could see far enough, he'd be looking at the Indian ocean and maybe the coast of East Africa,. Zanzibar… or Mombasa. That made him stop in his tracks. For all the planes, trains and subway cars, this was a moment for him. He considered the sheer size of the globe he'd been forced to traverse.

He felt remote but also free. It was possible here that news might get to him a day late. He liked that feeling.

Chapter 4 – Underworld

The Hawthorne Principle

Elton Mayo should be feted in business circles as a role model for those who never give up. The Australian psychologist was in his forties and two-thirds of the way through his life when he moved to the USA. He went from the University of Pennsylvania to Harvard. It was while at Harvard that he got involved in roughly 30 years of experiments at the Hawthorne factory outside Chicago. There were 45,000 people working in the factory. Roughly the number of people that fit in a midsized football ground in England. They were making telephone equipment. He set an assembly line aside and observed the workers under different conditions. He was delighted to see production go up when he allowed them to set their own working conditions. He then let them adjust the heat and air-flow. Production rose. Plan the timing of your shifts? More phone boxes are produced. And on it went. Ever the scientist, Mayo realised he need a control. So, he made them work unsociable hours. Production still increased. *He opened the windows in winter.* More *telephone switching boxes were made. Confounded, the 30-year research project did give science one vital concept: The Hawthorne Principle – If people are being observed attentively, they work harder.*

Meanwhile, more than a century later, an L-train and a few buses will get you to the site of the Hawthorne factory in Cicero, Illinois. Only one tower is left of the original structure. The rest is car park, and a Hooters.

Chris stood in his hotel room and looked out to sea. His thoughts drifted to Kevin, the family dog. Amidst all the changes of the past 18 months, Chris hadn't really mourned the long-time family pet. As is usual, Kevin was acquired at the behest of the children. They promised to love it and look after it for ever! And there started Chris' close and symbiotic relationship with Kevin. They walked together. They talked. Kevin less than Chris, but they faced the world together.

Then Kevin chased an electric motorbike and lost. Only Chris' youngest child, Fleur, was at home to help Chris mourn. Together they had carefully made a paper-maché boat, a little bigger than a shoe box. They had built the hull to take Kevin's ashes. They drove to Richmond Lock, the first on the Thames, and got there just as the tide started going out. They let Kevin set sail into the heart of the city. No one knows how far he got.

Today, Bexley had a meeting planned in Perth.

He was meeting Henry Pickle to talk about mining. They had gotten to know each other when Prickle was in London with one of the big mining firms and the kids had swum together. The Australians take their swimming seriously, so the Pickle girls far outpaced the Bexley children. But poolside was good for chatting.

Pickle had gone into investments and claims when he returned to Oz. It had gone well. Pickle didn't need to work anymore. They met at a coffee shop close to Bexley's hotel. It was nondescript but contained. There was only one entrance, the kitchen was open, and the staff could all be seen at all times. Henry had suggested it.

When Bex arrived, Henry Pickle was there already. Sitting in the middle of the café but with his back against the wall, facing the door. He looked older, but more expensive. His shoes, haircut, a fresh shave... all made Bexley wish he'd brushed his hair this morning.

"Good morning, sir." He said as he approached Pickle.

"Well, hello, young man! How the devil are you?" Pickle stood and gave him a great, squishy bear-hug. Bex feared for his brittle bones.

"I am well. All the better for seeing you."

"We haven't aged a bit, have we old boy!"

"You look magnificent. I look like my aunt Joan."

"Rubbish, you look like a whippet." It wasn't the first time Chris had heard that.

"Well, they haven't had me destroyed yet." It also wasn't the first time he'd replied thus.

They talked idly about their kids, their ex-wives and the state of their work… or in Henry's case the lack thereof.

"What brings a chap like you here, Christopher?" Henry finally said.

"Well. Truth?" Bex said and Henry nodded. "I am not sure."

He paused for a while.

"A friend of mine has disappeared," Bexley continued. "And I am not sure where she is, but I'd like to find her. I think the answer is going to be here somewhere."

"Have you spoken to the police…" Henry paused, and his eyes flickered. "Oh. I see. Yes, you have, but you don't think they'll find her?"

Bexley swallowed. He'd got it in one. "That's more or less it, Henry."

"We'll I'm not a detective. Or a missing persons expert. What can I do?"

"I just want to better understand aspects of the industry, Henry. And I think you'll feel free to give me the unvarnished truth." Henry nodded and looked up at the door. Not for the first time. He scanned the room again. "I think we might need some more coffee, darling?" Pickle said to the passing waitress.

Henry pulled out a pen while the hot drinks were being prepared and wrote a few notes to himself in a small booklet he produced. Seemingly to structure his thoughts.

"Let me start by putting Australia into a slightly different context than you might have heard before. This country is a series of little settlements on the water. Those settlements surround a giant, unliveable desert. There are less than 27 million people here. That's a lot less than California. A few more than Texas. But Australia *is* a big place. There are less than 4 people per square kilometre. A lot less than that if you use your fancy Imperial system."

"The birth rate is below break even. Even with immigration, we are not growing. And why would we. We do good marketing in the UK, but the kids who come here to live the life always go home. Sometimes they take an Aussie with them."

"So, what do we have? Kylie? MasterChef? Priscilla Queen of the Desert? That won't get us far. But we do have minerals. The earth here, that is so bloody inhospitable, is actually overflowing with stuff that you guys need... and more importantly our Asian neighbours. It's 4,200 clicks from Darwin to Hong

Kong. That's where the people are. There are fifty-five times as many people in China as there are here in Oz. And those people in China need our rocks."

"Generally speaking, we are happy to sell them. But at the same time, we have started to realise that we can make more money off the rocks if we do more of the processing – refining, buffing, polishing – here. And our friends who run the People's Republic don't like that. As a result, we are having some argy-bargy from time to time."

"That's all good. But just like Ukraine found out that Russians didn't like having to form an orderly queue, the good people of *La Chine* may prove too impatient for us."

Bex cut in. "You're not talking a war?" The current land wars in Europe had seemed impossible about 18 months ago, so Chris was ready for anything. The hostilities of south-east Asia was not a course he'd taken in university.

"No, no, no. Nothing that formal. But we are at war already." Pickle smiled and looked around the café, then the street. "This place is already crawling with spies." He smiled again and put his hands on the table. "I know that sounds fanciful. But there are lots of interested parties, all over the world, who want to know what's happening. Who want to buy a rock for less than the other guy. Who may even want to upset the supply chains for 'strategic' reasons." Henry Pickle was even kind enough to do half an 'air-quote' for Bex.

He paused to let it sink in. He checked his notes and seemed satisfied. He closed the booklet and put it back in his jacket pocket.

"Okay. I think I've got that. But let me add something else... what can you tell me about Lithium?"

Henry blinked a few times at Bexley. Then he smiled.

"Do you have lunch plans?" Pickle asked. "Darling?" he said again as he flagged down the waitress and reached again for his notebook.

They didn't move, but they did order.

Prickle again wrote a few short notes, and then breathed in deeply.

"Right. What do you know about Lithium?"

"I know more than I did a few days ago. I know about the metal, its instability, the many uses... who knew about air conditioning and dry cleaning? But what I don't know enough about is the strategic importance, the current state of production, the black market... I think this is connected to my friend having disappeared... and maybe why I am in Australia..."

"Okay, I think I know what we're talking about now." Pickle shifted in his seat, "tell me this… How much of this does your Canadian friend know?"

"What Canadian friend?" Bex was genuinely surprised.

"The lady you landed with…"

It was Bexley's turn to blink. "The *what*? I came alone." Pause.

"I don't know man. This is a small country. Like I said. I hear stuff."

Bexley looked around slowly now. He wasn't anywhere near as subtle at Pickle. When Bex looked at people they looked back at him, a slight question in their faces.

"Christ," he said quietly. "Okay, I will come back to my shadow… a woman you say? *Jesus.* But let's stick to lithium for now. What can you tell me?"

"I can tell you I am happy that I got out of mining when I did. The story can be simply stated: Australia has lithium. China does not have enough. We do not have the biggest reserves. But we do have some of the most accessible supply. And we have a stable government, etc. Plus, we are close to Xi Jinping and his mates… and they are all 'his mates'. By *close* though, I mean geographically. The Wendi Deng Offensive, as we call it here, was not a monster of a success. Even the kids she had with Uncle Rupert have left the region."

The Australian press baron, Ruport Murdoch, married the Chinese entrepreneur Wendi Deng in 1999. They divorced in 2013. Deng changed her name as a child to Wendi, from Wenge, which means *Cultural Revolution*. She went to the USA to study on a student visa and ended up getting an MBA from Yale. Although Deng and Murdoch have two daughters together, none of them live anywhere near China.

In a different part of town Lulu was getting a similar story. Although from a more juridical angle.

"Do you make this rosé here?" she was shouting into the house from the poolside. "I don't mean in this house. I mean in *Austr-AH-lia*. Of course, you do," she answered her own question. Her hosts were busy inside the bungalow, so she was having to talk to herself. "Well, I like it. I think I'll take some home. But... come back. I have more questions. Dammit." She flipped over like an egg in a fry pan. Time to cook the other side.

Wendy came back out carrying a doll by its foot. She sat down near Lulu, looked at the doll blankly and placed it by her chair.

"So, you know what Lithium is, but do you want to know how the 'Lithium Economy' works?" Wendy supplied the air-quotes this time.

Lulu opened her eyes. "There's a *Lithium Economy*?"

"Well, no, I kind of made up that term. But I think it will catch on." Wendy seemed apologetic. "It is everywhere, lithium, but the need for it is increasing at a crazy rate. It's not something that we have really dealt with. There have been no Channel 3 exposés. It almost seems like a conspiracy of silence." She paused. "If we believed in conspiracies," Wendy said to herself. "Which we don't. But, what I do think is happening, is that the media hasn't really caught on to the story and no one involved in the Lithium Economy – TM – wants to draw attention to it."

Georgia came and joined them, carrying another bottle of rosé.

"I'm just talking about the Lithium Economy…"

"Yea, that will never catch on," Georgia said. Wendy gave her a long stare.

"Anyway, the truth is that large companies and national government – sometimes even regional governments – looking for a financial leg up, are all out in the field trying to influence the prospecting… purchasing… mining…refining… and distribution of lithium. When it was all Duracells, and the occasional nuclear bomb, there was more than enough to go around. Although it was still expensive. Now, though, people are even attaching battery packs to their house to gather and store their own thermal and solar energy." Wendy turned to Georgia. "That's not even a niche thing anymore. They are making household battery packs that are designed by like Tom Ford, to accessorise your house."

"She's not fucking with you," Georgia said.

"So, who are all these people on the ground that you referred to?" Lulu asked.

"The common term these days seems to be 'State Actors'. We have gotten used to that with the situation in Ukraine, but it makes sense here," Wendy went on. "They are often paid for by a dubious Commercial Department budget, in an Embassy or High Commission. And then the actual people tend to be old private eyes, or former journalists, who get paid, eventually, and in a round-about way by large corporations."

Georgia picked up the explanation. "If they were written about in the media, it would be to say they are Chinese agents, or Russian FSB members. But that would be a massive oversimplification. There are probably more American, French and German-sponsored actors in Australia right now than Russian. It's like a mad rave for internationally sponsored spies."

"How do you know all this?" Lulu asked. "No to be disrespectful, but you are lawyers…"

"Ha. Yes. Who do you think hires the big law firms here? And what do you think we're asked to do? We work for the miners. We work for the embassies. We get people into the country. We get them out quickly, when they get caught. We help the companies put together the complex ownership structures and we help them delay having to report findings."

"But, Lulu, we are still nice people," Wendy interjected with a look of mock surprise.

Georgia carried on. "In many ways it was always this way. But with this chemical, lithium, the implications of poorly managed Health and Safety, or foreign acts of sabotage, are so much higher than with Iron Ore, Copper or even our famous pink Diamonds. This stuff is – to coin a phrase – deadly. Just grabbing a hand-full of lithium can kill you."

Wendy came back into the conversation. "So, there is one industry that is easy to quantify. You can go to StatsOz and get the number of people who work in it. You can look at tonnes shipped and see where the lithium is going. But that's only half of the story."

"We don't know," Georgia said. "It could only be 20% of the story."

"Okay," Lulu said. "It sounds like my research was a bit flawed. Or perhaps not quite deep enough…"

"Have you ever been to a mine?" Wendy pulled out her mobile phone and typed a few words into Google maps. She pinched and pushed and pressed on the satellite setting. "This is what it looks like." She held up her phone for Lulu to see.

"Sheee-it." Lulu said squinting into the sun. "That looks like the surface of the moon."

"Yup. But we like to call it Western Australia."

♒

Coffee had turned into lunch, which then included some alcohol. Bex had walked the short way home in the sun. It was hot. For the winter. He made it into the air-conditioning of the hotel lobby and sat down with a thump on one of the round tuxedo sofas in the lobby.

After a minute as he was about to raise himself to make the final trek to his room, he heard a clear voice. "Mr Bexley, you are asking a lot of questions."

"Pardon me?" Bex looked around, but the woman has her back to him. She was slight with a short bob of black hair. He would have had to have gotten up and walked around the sofa to get to her. "Who are you?"

"I'm just here to say that you don't need to get involved. That's what I want to say. You 'don't have a dog in this fight'. I think that's how you say it?" It was an odd expression, made more odd by the woman's accent.

"Okay." Bex said. "I'm not sure what I am doing, but can you tell me who I am upsetting?"

"It might be easier to tell you who you are not upsetting, Christopher. I think you'd be better back in Knightsbridge."

Chris got to his feet and turned around. But there was no one there. The only movement he could see what a door closing behind reception.

He went to the door of the hotel and looked out into the street. He could see nothing out of the ordinary. He went back to the hotel lobby and sat down again. This time in the seat that the woman must have been sitting in. He looked out. He could see nothing interesting.

He checked his pocket for his room key. And then he went back up to his room and closed the bathroom door. He turned on the tap in the sink and the shower and he pulled out his mobile phone. It was a new one. Hatch had taken his old phone. But he switched off the Wi-Fi and opened WhatsApp just the same.

"Hello Mrs Springer," he said. "How are you? What time is it there? I am sorry is it very early."

"It is time to do some work, Christopher. What can I help with?"

"I think I'm going to need some new accommodation. And maybe some new clothes..."

"I can help with a new residence," the Austrian replied, "but you'll need to do your own fashion purchases."

♒

"I was home-schooled too, you know." Lulu was in the back of Wendy and Georgia's giant Land Rover with one of their daughters on each side.

"No!" said Poppy, the younger one.

"No way!" said Sabrina. "Just like her!"

"Yes, way," said Lulu in an artificially high voice. "And... I am part Asian too. Not Filipina like Olivia Rodrigo, but I am part Japanese. I am!"

"Wow. You're like sisters," Sabrina said. "Do you know her?"

"No," said Lulu with a drop of her shoulders and a big sigh. "I can't even sing. Or... I can, but you won't like the sound of it."

"Can you dance though?!" asked Poppy, unwilling to give up. "Can you dance like Olivia Rodrigo?"

“Um, I don’t know.” Lulu admitted. “Does she dance? You’re starting to get to the limits of my knowledge.”

“I thought you said you were a super-fan?” Sabrina said rudely.

“That’s enough young ladies. Lulu is not here to amuse you.”

“But we DO like her,” Poppy said leaning into Lulu.

The car pulled up and they got out into the city streets of Perth. They had parked beside Kings Park, the water visible over the green grass and trees. When a police car pulled up beside them. The window rolled down and the siren sounded once in a weak blast.

“Lulu Downs?” She turned around and pushed the two girls towards their mums. “You are going to need to come with us…”

♒

The seaside shop is the same everywhere in the world, Bex thought to himself. I could be in Margate, or beautiful downtown Ramsgate. Brighton. New Jersey. Anywhere.

He was standing inside a shop just off the high street. There were children’s fishing nets hanging outside. Inflatable animals, cheap towels, wet suits, snorkels, Havaianas by the bundle. He'd found a pair of shorts that didn't show off his knobbly knees, and a t-shirt that said something about sea, sand and speed, but the colours weren't too flashy. He had his wide-brimmed hat with him but he bought one in a lighter shade as well, a slightly floppier cut. He couldn't imagine wearing open-toed shoes, so he'd bought some Crocs in a tank-coloured green. He was uncomfortable. But comfortable.

He left the shop feeling better. A bag of his old clothes, Uniqlo specials, in his hand.

Then a car slowed down beside him, and a bored looking policeman hung his hear out the window. "Bexley," the man said. It didn't seem to be either a question or an accusation. It was just a statement.

"No," Chris said "Soy un vaquero ... de la gente de los caballos..."

"Yea. Just get in the car."

"Okay." He opened the back door and clambered in.

Chapter 5 – Bringing up the dead

The hierarchy of needs

It is clear that Abraham Maslow had some of his own demons. His family had fled Czarist forces in Kyiv for the streets of Brooklyn. When they got there they were still harassed by antisemitic gangs. He had a life-long antipathy for his mother. Nonetheless young Abraham married his first cousin Bertha, and although he believed men should be strong and fit, he never convinced his own body to cooperate. He died, while out for a run, aged 62.

Maslow was a positivist. *His life's work primarily revolved around the need he perceived for humans to achieve self-actualisation. He was a pioneer of psychological health. Although he wasn't particularly interested in organisations – let alone businesses – Maslow's Hierarchy of Needs is a favourite model of Human Resources professionals the world over. He proposed that each need had to be met before the next could be tackled. He listed them as Physiological, then Safety, then Love, and then Esteem, before you could reach Self-Actualisation.*

(For extra points: Harvard psychologist and LSD-guru Timothy Leary built on Maslow's five and

created eight. The last three involved living extra-terrestrially.)

The business papers were clear, the American Treasury Secretary's visit to China was a success. She was still there, but Margaret Adams had already both charmed and warned the Chinese officials. She assured them that the new measures extolled by President Biden, were going to protect America from too heavy a reliance on foreign (particularly) Chinese technology. But that this was not going to be a game changer. Chinese businesses could expect to carry on as before. The screening would be highly targeted. Which sounded both reassuring and a bit of a warning.

In fairness to the home of the bald eagle, the Chinese had not covered themselves in glory lately, with wandering spy balloons, dodgy technology installed in proposed US infrastructure, and failing to make any meaningful connection in the Russia-Ukraine business. Viewed from a different perspective, with less fear and more time to reflect, it could all look like the work of Inspector Clouseau.

Margaret Adams was a force to be reckoned with too. She knew more about China and the Chinese than the locals ever expected an American to. She managed her team and her agenda masterfully. Never being rude but also not doing what she was told at every turn. It's often a surprise to hear just how many senior US officials actually went to a little red schoolhouse as children. China was no longer a mysterious country.

Almost directly on the other side of the globe, in Jamaica, there was a meeting of the International Seabed Authority taking place. This obscure organisation was not yet 30 years old. It had been set up to manage, or at least try to protect, more than half of the world's ocean floor that is not claimed or managed by an adjoining nation. Even 30 years ago this might have seemed like an esoteric and unnecessary organisation. Who can be bothered to go to the bottom of the ocean? Even looking at old wrecks had recently become less fashionable.

However, in the 2020s the minerals on the sea floor were looking more and more attractive. Particularly with the exponentially growing demand for batteries. There's Lithium out there.

There were 168 member states at the meeting, which was pretty good in a world where there are only 195. (About 15 of those states have fewer than 100,000 people in them.)

The hotel and hospitality business in Kingston, Jamaica hadn't seen this much action in many, many years. No nation appeared without a sizable entourage. (There were 15 people from Malta.) Meaning that hotels were stretched. Restaurants bursting and all the other goods and services – legal and illegal – were being tested to the limits. Out of necessity, rather than extravagance, some teams were flying in and out from neighbouring islands. And some were set up in rented super-yachts parked in bays and harbours. However, with so much else going on in the world, the 14th meeting of the International Seabed Authority was not drawing the attention of any notable media outlets.

The delegates were there to agree the first set of operating guidelines for the nascent sea-floor exploitation business. The Russians, who were short on cash, had led the dredging of the sea just off Canada's coastal water for fish. Their vessels, that looked like giant ploughs, had dragged the seabed like a thresher and simply spat back out the coral, flora and fauna that it didn't think could be eaten, leaving a dump of broken matter in its wake. In Jamaica, they were leading an informal, rag-tag alliance that included South Korea, Norway, Venezuela, South Africa and China, who were anxious to just get on with the exploitation. (Norway knew well that there is money to be made underwater.)

The pro-sea-mining camp could argue compellingly that the world was short of copper and cobalt, which are so critical to modern electronics. Without these, they argued, the growing tribes of people who want heat and light at the flick of a switch were going to be sitting in the cold and dark. Their TVs and laptops would be dead.

On the other side of the table were reticent lawyers in well-tailored suits who saw this as their chance to write laws like those created for space travel. The 'dreamers' felt that this could be a sea-bed Magna Carta for this whole new, watery would. That feeling can make you giddy as you hold the pen over paper.

They were well supported though. Fighting in this corner were the diplomatic heavyweights of France and Germany and the gifted local team captains, Chile. They were worried that a poorly managed approach could lead to permanent damage to an ecosystem that is barely understood. They had history on their side. Humans hadn't made a good fist of the environment above sea-level, why should they be trusted with the remaining 71% of the Earth's surface?

However, through the arcane voting system that the ISA was stuck with, they would need a 2/3rds majority to reject the plans to open up the sea to more mining.

Stand by the sea on any coast in China and you will be looking out at some of the biggest concentration of mineral deposits in the world: Polymetallic peaks, cobalt-rich valleys and plains of sulphides just lying around, not even being coy.

Additionally, in Jamaica there were developers, who were making themselves known. They were gearing up to start mining the sea in 18-months' time. The starters pistol had already gone off. In Kingston the delegates had a last chance to call a false-start.

All of this activity was drawing the diplomatic classes, regulators, legislators, agitators and innovators from different corners of the world. Journalists who cover these matters – mining and/or China – were engaged in Jamaica. No one was interested in what was happening to an awkward couple of foreigners in Western Australia.

When the police car door opened, and Lulu Tanaka-Brown was pushed in beside Christopher Bexley, he felt that she looked familiar. He recognised the strange duck-footed walk, the wide-leg capri trousers. The glasses and the rosy cheeks set on a round, happy face.

Today though she was looking a little more dangerous. There was an aura of anger about her that made him fearful. He looked straight ahead.

The two louts who had picked them up were back in the front seat and talking banalities to each other. Their words could only be imagined through the clear plastic partition that separated front from back seat of the German car.

Eventually Lulu spoke to Bexley:

“Please tell me you’re a counterfeiter, not a paedophile.”

Bexley looked at her blankly. “I’m a management consultant.”

He realised that sounded defensive, so he tried to sound friendlier. “I don’t know what I am doing here. Are you the Canadian lady that I am meant to be in Australia with?”

“Oh, you’re what the locals call a Pom,” she said accusingly. The followed that with. “I’m not here with anyone. Did you not know it was a *bring-your-own-woman* event?”

“I am not even sure what I am doing in the back of this car. I haven’t broken any laws.” His confusion was real. “I always pay my taxes on time,” he said plaintively.

There was a pause. Lulu's anger seemed to steam up the window on her side of the police car.

"The Australians aren't the most hospitable people, are they?" She said finally. "These guys are mouth-breathers."

"I sensed they were hoping for a bit of resistance."

"Amen. Good call to avoid that. They like a bit of self-defence..."

"What have you done to get here? Are you the murderer?" Bexley tried to sound defiant.

"I am not. Or... if I am, they don't know anything about it," she turned and gave Bexley a smile.

"What is your name?"

"I am Lulu. You?"

"Bexley. Christopher Bexley."

"Oh good. May I call you Chip?"

"No, you may not," Bex looked horrified, but he gathered himself. "Unless I can call you Lucinda?"

"I've been called worse. So, no, I wouldn't kill you. But I might hurt you a lot. I am Lulu Tanaka-Brown. I know, it's a mouthful. My parents were cruel."

Bexley found her charming, and frightening. She seemed a fairly benign force. Although she clearly was a force of something. As his kids might say, she had a good vibe.

They had arrived at the police station. It seemed to have been built to look like a Gothic Batman set. Ionic columns holding up a heavy dome. They were carted inside and placed together in a cell. "The Detectives will be here shortly to talk to you separately. You're on the docket for a chat with Killer Cahill..." The policemen both laughed with a full sneer. Undoubtedly something they'd practiced in the mirror.

Lulu sat down with a deep sigh. She looked at Bexley. "I'm pretty sure Cahill gets called that because he used to work in an abattoir."

Bexley laughed. "That would still make him good with blood. I'd like to think he is just a good batsman. He can see out the innings, without giving away another wicket."

Lulu looked at him in confusion.

"Okay Chip. What are we going to do?"

"First of all, you're going to stop calling me Chip. I can handle Chris, Christo or Bex. But not Chip. You Americans can be really annoying with your nicknames."

"Touché," the Canadian replied.

She re-grouped and look at him again. "So, shall we get our stories straight before Killer comes in? Why are you in Perth, Bex?"

"I'm here for The Ashes. Are you a cricket fan Lulu."

"No. No, I am not Chris," she said. "But I do know that the Ashes are being contested in the UK at the moment. You might have bought a bad travel package. Not all of us Colonials are thick, you know. I have a sense of why you are here, and I think maybe we should compare notes, but I also recognise that this is not the place to do that. So, when these guys let us go, in the next half hour, let us sit down and compare notes. I think it may be useful for both of us."

Bex thought for a few moments and slowly said, "I'm not really sure what I am doing here, so maybe you can fill me in at that time too?" He paused again, "Mais, peut-etre on devrais parlé en français ?"

Lulu smiled. The door opened and Killer Cahill came in.

Lulu laughed. Killer looked at her curiously. "Good morning, I am Derek Cahill. And I have been asked to speak to you. You are Chris Bexley and Lulu Tanaka-Brown?"

"Correct."

"Yes," Lulu jumped in. "Are we being held here? Are charges pending? Is anyone able to tell us what those charges are?"

"No. No. And No. But I don't think you should go until we have been able to talk. If you don't mind. I don't have much to ask, but I do have a few things…."

"Okay, but can you make it quick. As you can see, Mr Baxter and I are very busy people…"

"Bexley," Chris said crisply.

Cahill shook his head and smiled. "We're on the same side here. I grew up near a mine in Scotland. My dad and three uncles were all miners. I know a surprising amount about the business. And I like people… people like you. I am here to help. I have been hired by the international mining association to keep an eye out for you… and, to be completely honest, to look for Justine. Which I think is what you are doing as well."

Bexley and Lulu looked at each other. They were.

Lulu raised her hand high like an overachieving schoolgirl. "Sir? Killer?"

"Yes, Lulu?"

"I have two questions. Number one: Why are you in a police station in Australia? You're clearly not a local. And… Two: Can we talk about this over pizza and a beer outside this hideous building?"

"Yes. To both of those. Let me fulfil my contract first though. I need you to answer some questions for me first. One, Chris, why are you travelling as Nicolai Mikhnevich from Belarus?"

Chris and Lulu exchanged curious looks. "I can explain," said Chris, "but I'd rather not do it here."

"And Lulu," Cahill continued, "do you think that no one in Australia knows that you work for See-Cist?"

Lulu replied sharply: "As you fully well know, it is CSIS, pronounced See-Sis. An acronym for Canadian Security Intelligence Services. *Nous sommes des espions*," she said for Chris' benefit. She added an awkward wink as an afterthought.

"The question I need to ask you," Cahill said, "is what do you know about Holstium?"

"What?" Bexley said. "Hol-ski-am?"

"Holstium," Cahil corrected and looked at Lulu. "What do you know?"

"I know it doesn't really exist," she said quickly. "It's an idea that doesn't work. There is no 'Holstium', it is a non-thing."

Cahill picked up his papers and turned to the mirror in the room. He nodded and headed for the door. "Okay, let's go get pizzas. I think we've done enough here."

Bexley looked at Lulu quizzically. She went on in a quiet voice. "Holstium is a synthetic lithium. Or that's the theory. But it's not really anything. I was meant to be working on it in my last job, but I figured out it was just a big, fat nothing. That's what I was meant to find out. And I did. But I also wasn't meant to find that out… because someone…" And here she raised her voice and looked at Cahill, "SOMEONE BLEW THE WHOLE FUCKING PLACE UP!"

Cahill paused and looked at her. He was easily 6' 5", he looked like he cut his own hair and his nose that was a prominent feature. "It wasn't me."

"I know it wasn't you. But I'd like to know who it was… and why they wanted me to be in there at the time…"

They checked out of the Australian police station and headed out on the streets of Perth.

♒

The three expats compared notes, made plans and told ridiculous stories over food.

It wasn't totally easy. Lulu knew nothing about football. Cahill knew nothing about ice hockey, and Bex seemed only interested in jogging and cricket. But they had a lot in common, nonetheless. A neutral observer might also say they all also had a bit too much faith that everything would turn out okay in the end. Cautious optimism, they'd say. Other might call it wishful thinking

Cahill spoke to them with great fluidity about the declining Chinese economy. He explained that the coming Chinese recession was not something that the Central Committee were really experienced with. The Electric Vehicle market was growing too fast. The Chinese were losing their edge. At the heart of all this – and central to the rush to address climate change – was the need for more lithium. The element was key to the battery market and instrumental in moving the world towards renewable energy. But it was in short supply. Lulu would jump in occasionally with some stats, but Cahill clearly had the upper hand when it came to talking about China and renewable energy.

China aren't really in favour of renewable energy, he explained. They have invested a lot in securing consistent supplies of fossil fuels from home and from friendly nations.

When the group broke up, they all shared their plans for next steps. Bexley was keen to get on a plane, but Lulu insisted they go together now ("save on taxis") and she had some background to do before they could leave. Mrs Springer was going to book them tickets for the following evening. John Hatch had left his credit card details, she explained.

This was all fine and well for Lulu, who said she was going back to the pool and the rosé for another day. Chris was less well prepared. Springer had found him an AirBnB with a view of the ocean – almost. She'd had his bags moved. But he was still wandering around looking like a middle-aged tourist in mid-mid-life crisis. He wanted to lie down. He wasn't feeling too comfortable in Australia anymore. The good people of Perth hadn't endeared themselves to him yet. He texted Andrea in London

When he got back to his room he checked his watch, set up his laptop, made a cup of tea and dialled into a call with his psychotherapist.

"Hello, Chris. This is a change. I've never seen you on a screen before."

"Andrea, thank you. I appreciate you taking the time to speak to me."

They did a quick exercise to 'check-in'.

"So, Chris... what's going on in your world?"

Chris paused and looked for a twinge of a smile from Andrea Spino. He thought he saw one. "Hey," he said, "that's my line."

Spino laughed. "I am sorry, I know. I was just trying it on. I like it."

"This is serious stuff, Andrea."

"I know, I know... what's on your list today."

"It's just one thing."

"Oh?"

"I think I am losing my mind."

"Oh!"

"I am struggling to keep up both physically and emotionally. I know I am not a young man. But I am totally exhausted. I can't stop my brain working, but meanwhile my body is crying 'foul!' I am shaking. I think I may be trying to be something I am not. I don't know how I get into these situations. I like peace and quiet. I like routine. I don't LIKE people. I would rather be at home... doing nothing. Getting paid for it, and going to bed with some Ovaltine."

"You like Ovaltine?"

"It's a figure of speech Andrea, stay with me."

"I am. Where are you. That doesn't look like the Thames behind you Chris."

"It doesn't matter where I am. I am not at home."

"We'll it's 7:18 in the morning here. I am not normally working at this time of day. So, it's clearly not Norwich. Are you off on another adventure...?"

"Christ. Yes. I guess I am," Bexley paused.

"Well, that's going to have something to do with it. It doesn't matter if it's the first day at kindergarten, a new job, or walking into the Legion for the first time. Doing new things is hard. At any age. You've been through a lot of change here, at home, in London, recently. Don't be surprised if you get tired doing new things. How about this? What new things have you done in the last 24 hours?"

Bexley laughed. "Oh, Andrea, I wouldn't know where to start."

"Are you hating every minute of it?"

Bexley paused and thought. Andrea let the thinking time pass. "No. I am not hating it. Adrenaline is good, even at my age. I am finding it invigorating. But I am still feeling very much apart from it. Like I am standing above. Sometimes I am saying and doing things and I wonder who is doing that. It doesn't feel like me."

Andrea just looked at him. Bex wondered sometimes if the psychologist and schoolteachers were both taught how to show that you disappointment them. It was a look of someone recognising failure. Bex wasn't sure really what his resting-face looked like. He was pretty sure Andrea's was better.

"I am wired. That's what I feel. I feel like I am sitting on a live current. I had a long flight out here and I couldn't settle. I take a long time to fall asleep. It's not helped by being in a different room every night," he said, more to himself than to the therapist.

"But, I also feel very isolated. How can I be in the midst of hundreds... thousands of people... filled with adrenaline and... still feel very much alone and removed?" He paused, not realising that was what he was calling about. "Is that normal?"

"Isolation? Feelings of being apart from others? Chris, I think you read some literature and philosophy at university. You are talking about the core issue of the 'human condition'. We are all alone, but also, we are part of the greater whole. How many people have you interacted with today? Why have you spoken with?"

"Lots of people. Too many people..."

"*L'enfer c'est les autres*. Hell is other people, right?"

"Andrea, are you quoting Sartre at me? It's a bit early in your day."

"It's never too early for a bit of existentialism. But I'm not a great believer. We talked about this in the past." The therapist set himself in his seat, seemingly ready to say something longer. "You remember when we talked about sports in the past? You were a rugby player, right?"

"I was a fast runner, who didn't like getting tackled. It served its purposes."

"And what happened when you got tackled?"

"It hurt."

"What was the expression you used? For when someone tackled you in rugby? You said they 'left something on you'. Do you remember that? I like that idea.... Tell me Chris who has left something on you this week, this past day? Who have you left something on? Who have you touched, and impacted, and changed the course of?"

"Ah. I think I get it."

"And if you're not sleeping, or you're wired, it's probably because you can't close down the part of your brain that is still making sense of it all. Your hard drive is still defragging, while you are awake. That's a way of thinking about it…"

"I think that is right. I can see that. But what can I do about it? How can I get off this particular ride?"

"Meditate?"

"Oh, no. I tried. I am rubbish. I can't do that."

"You can, I know you can, because I have seen you do it. At the start of our sessions."

There was a long pause.

Andrea was happy just to leave it there.

"Okay. Thanks Andrea. I think I get it."

"Can I go back to bed now?"

"Yes. Thank you. Thank you."

"Bye."

Lulu had her iPad with her by the pool. She had aviator glasses that she knew made her look cool. And she was still squinting at the screen. She was on the wi-fi and on a secure line. VPN Extra.

Subject: Data request

CLASSIFIED & CONFIDENTIAL

I'd like to request a summary file on A. Jamieson Johnston, deceased. Topline information, resume.

Also, files from early life 1950s. Any travel to the East. Any known contacts or collaborators from that time.

Send by secure post with online access only.

Thanks much, LMB

She switched off the tablet and reached for her rosé. She had some time now. Off the clock.

♒

Bob Lang drove off the Paoli Turnpike on to the side road. He turned down a dirt track over the ditch that ran along the road, and into a larger grass and gravel parking lot. There were a few cars there and at the far side of the informal space was an old wood frame building. There was faded signs outside that read: "COFFEE" and "ICE CREAM".

He pulled his car over, opened the door and went to look in the trunk. There wasn't much there, but he adjusted it anyway to make room in the centre of the space for more cargo. Then he went into the diner. The noise, smoke and odours inside the building belied the quiet outside. There were a few people on video calls, on their phones or on laptops and tablets. They were talking at an unnatural volume, as if to make up the space between the café and the people at home. There were people concentrating heavily on the food and drink in front of them. A few seeking answers at the bottom of a coffee cup. And there were people standing around drinking a quick espresso and chatting to a friend or colleague before going on to the job.

When Bob arrived, there was a booth ready for him. He smiled at a few people and quietly, though carefully, took his seat. A waiter came over to him and addressed him quickly in Mandarin. There was nodding, and a bow, and the server scurried off again.

A seasoned observer might have noticed two or three people catch each other's eyes. Then one stepped forward in silent agreement, and slid into the booth across from Lang. There was a brief exchange of pleasantries and then a zip-lock bag of tiny USB sticks appeared and was slid across the table. It was followed by a larger object, wrapped in newsprint. A ream of paper, or so. The emissary slipped away. As a cup of coffee arrived, Bob Lang got up from his seat and carried the paper and plastic bag to the trunk of his car. He then returned to his seat.

A similar scene played out three more times, around food arriving, being consumed and the waiter receiving payment and a $10 note on the table.

And then Lang was gone.

Lulu and Bex met up again at Perth Airport. Derek 'Killer' Cahill had given them an important tip: A name and a place where they were might just find Justine Jurys. Cahill explained that there was some "noise in the system" suggesting that she was being taken to Silver Peak, Nevada. Although it is a place with a lovely name, Cahill said that it was anything but. The town was deep in the Nevada desert and had little to show for itself. Except for its cobalt lakes. These aquamarine, blue and turquoise shallow ponds were lithium filtering bays. They are visible from space. Clearly identifiable on Google Earth.

Silver Peak has pride of place in the mining community as a location that was driving innovation. It was one of Justine's mines. No one knew for sure what Justine and her colleagues were doing at Silver Peak, but quite a few were keen to find out. There were many rumours. Some had even made it into print. They were simulating lithium, some said. Like the famous Holstium that Lulu had already said didn't exist. Others said that it was about cloning the existing minerals, making more out of what they already had, through some chemical sleight of hand. Some felt that they were simply extricating it from water faster than others could. This seemed the most likely. But whatever it was the market was interested and the company's share price had been having a good run for almost two years now.

Cahill promised to put them in touch with a legend in the area and in the biochemical world. Her name was Hazer Mayberry. Killer had warned that she was a bit eccentric but promised that she would see them. He said he'd get in touch with her while they travelled. He'd share the necessary background with her too.

Bex and Lulu boarded the flight in Perth. The first stop was Melbourne. Then Los Angeles. And finally, Las Vegas. Hazel was to be found in the suburb of Enterprise, Nevada. In all it would take them 25 hours of travel time. Sleep was recommended.

Chris settled into his seat. An aisle seat. Lulu was already sitting in the lotus position beside him, a spring in her seat. He closed his eyes. He breathed in through his nose, counting to eight. Then out through his mouth, through a ten-count. After a few minutes he was soundly asleep.

Lulu kicked off her shoes, crossed her legs under her, and opened her laptop. She found the secure file, entered her ID and began to scan it. There were lots of names she recognised. Stories from last century that still seemed relevant today.

♒

The Philadelphia Racquets Club is on 16th Street South. Roughly between City Hall and Rittenhouse Square. Its pedigree cannot be questioned. It is more than 130 years old, making it pre-Cambrian in American history terms. The initiation fee is almost $40,000. That entitles you to an annual membership payment of over $7,000 and a minimum food spend of another $800. The pool is very nice though.

Lang pulled up in front of the building. Parking his car easily in one of the open spots on an early summer morning. The Philadelphia elite had already gone to their houses in South Carolina, Ocala in Florida, Palms Spring or further afield… overseas.

He entered the club and greeted the two or three old members sitting patiently in the bright lit reception area. “Bob!” they said. He stopped to talk with each. Then he was up the marble staircase and into the bright red reading room. One of the attendants brought him a small cup of green tea. Bob took a few sips and placed a small brown envelope under the tea pot. The same attendant returned and deposited a small box the size of cigarette pack. Bob shook it and the microcassettes rattled inside. He smiled. He liked these little archaic items. They are easy to digitise but also easy to use, transport and they leave no online footprint. For a man who made his fortune in technology, Bob Lang was very reluctant to use too much tech.

He returned to his car and drove out into the Pennsylvanian sunshine.

The building was not uncomfortable. But it was peculiar. The polish concrete walls offset the elaborate Turkish carpets. The overstuffed Edwardian sofa and sclerotic end tables seemed at odds with the sharp blast of desert sunshine Justine could see coming through the high-up windows. If it was a holding cell, it was a nice one. Through one of the windows she could see water pouring down. She suspected, odd as it might seem, that she was below an infinity pool.

The door opened and Jack Clarke came in. They had met before, but Justine was only now feeling more like herself.

"Hello Jack. What have you got for me?"

"It's a Persian breakfast number. A sort of Shakshuka-like thing with a side dish of Adasi. You will like it. And it will make you regular."

Justine started. "Oh," she said. "Thanks. That's good to know."

"Jack, the temperature in here is very nice. Not too cool, but a lot cooler than out there." She said, "am I right in thinking there's a swimming pool above me?"

Jack placed the tray on her desk and looked around. "It's not a pool, really. There's no diving or snorkelling in it."

"But it is a body of water?"

"Yes."

"And why is that?"

"Um. I don't think you need to know that."

"Can I guess? Is it because thermal cameras can't see through water?"

Jack looked at her carefully. He smiled. "Got it in one," he said.

"But thermal cameras can't see through concrete either, my friend."

"Ah, yes, but concrete bunkers are more interesting than swimming pools."

Justine sighed. She rubbed her temples with her hands. Jack left quietly.

Chapter 6 – Silver Peak

Lewin's approach to change

Kurt Lewin was born in what is now Poland, at the end of the 19th century. He moved to Berlin in his teens and became involved in socialist causes, and the women's movement, while finding his way through the sciences at university. His curiosity took him into group dynamics and, from there, to becoming the father of organisational psychology. He created many important theories, including forcefield analysis, action research, and seminal work on group dynamic. However, the core theory of change management is most often ascribed to him as his crowning contribution. He suggested that change required an 'unfreezing' of behaviours, before a change of mindset could occur. And once that path had been successfully pursued, a 'freezing' was required again. John Kotter, Jeff Hiatt and others have built on this foundation.

"I've been on the Internet," Lulu said as Chris adjusted in his seat and poked at the cold plate of food that was on the tray in front of him.

"This Silver Peak is a mad place," she enthused. "At the last census there were 142 people living there." She looked around the cabin and did some quick mental maths. "That's half this cabin!" She paused and uncrossed her legs, putting them back in the seat well. "But it was also founded in 1864. It's the oldest mining town in Nevada. Lincoln was president. The Civil War was in full flow."

"In 1865 they discovered silver. The town grew. But by the 1920s, the mine was spent, and everything had shut down again. In the 40s the whole remaining town burnt to the ground."

"It almost never rains, but in the summer it can average more than 30C, and in the winter it drops below freezing. What a nightmare place."

"I bet there's a bar there like in *An Officer and a Gentleman*, or in *Roadhouse* with Patrick Swayze. Did you like that film, Bexley?" She tapped away on her keyboard.

Chris sniffed. "Loved it. Though I preferred his later work."

"Check this out," she said. "They even have a notorious murder. Charlie Kinkel III was working in the mine when his friend Jason caught him molesting his daughter and shot him in the head. Eww! He dumped him in a well…"

"Lulu. Can we stop now…"

Hazel saw them before they saw her. Lulu and Bex hadn't expected to be met at the airport. They might have washed up a bit, and made an effort, if they had. Hazel was holding a hand-drawn sign. It said: *Mr Bexley + LULU!* They realised it couldn't be anyone but them.

"I think I would have recognised you without the sign," she said as they shook her bird-like hand. "Derek gave me a pretty good description."

He'd not done the same for Lulu and Bex and they were caught off guard initially. Hazel had white-to-lemon coloured hair. It stood in punchy waves across her head, like patches of firm fishing line. She might have stood 5' 10' at one time but was nearing 5' now. Age had rounded her shoulders and doubled her back in on itself. She was wearing a thick knit jacket that Dior might have designed for a French winter in 1935. Vintage they'd call it now. Her makeup was liberally applied and the thinning of lips in old age had given no quarter to the blood-red application of an oval in the centre of her face. She leaned on a stick, which, on closer inspection, turned out to be an ancient 1-iron or putting cleek, gathered for an old golf bag. On her shoulder was Jackie Kennedy's Gucci handbag, and in her spare hand a disposable vape.

While talking over her shoulder about the history of the airport Hazel led them to the car park and to her giant, sky-blue Cadillac. In the UK it might have earned its own postal code.

"My goodness, Hazel. This is a big car," said Lulu admiringly.

"Oh, you think so? I feel like I should have gone for the 4-door version." She slammed their bags in the trunk and opened the passenger door. Pushing down the seat she motioned for Chris to get into the back. He looked at Lulu, who just smiled. But once in the back he found he had lots of white leather to lie on. There were no seatbelts in view. "I like to have a bit of power under the hood. And some distance between me and anything I am going to hit," she let out a hearty laugh. It sounded like an axe hitting a tree. Lulu laughed along.

♒

Jack Clarke pulled the Fiat 500 up to the doors of the Old Skool bar. It was the only commercial establishment in Silver Peak and not like most other bars. From the road it looked like a modest bungalow had been dragged to the curb. It had a wooden patio stretch around it with high wood benches around the outside. The words Old Skool were fastened to the outside wall, constructed from pieces of tree branch bolted together. The two Ls were shaped to look like boots – possibly.

Inside was a whole different feel. It was only just passed midday. When Jack opened the door to enter, a rush of stale, cool air flew past him. Inside there was no wall left bare. Two rows of empty beer bottles, all different, hung on shelves around the four walls. Below them were picture frames: old maps, fishing pictures, poems, blackboards... hanging less than an inch apart. From the floor in every corner rose wood-worked 'furniture'. A precarious looking desk, a model plane, an old dart board and more. The top of bar's serving counter was tiled with ivory, red and yellow tiles, making out geometric shapes, peace symbols, maybe a box, or a moon.

On a far wall was a framed mugshot of Jeff Taafe, famed for shooting that guy who messed with his daughter. He was a local hero. But not due for parole for some time yet.

Reg was behind the bar. 'The Professor', the locals called him, because he often read a book when no one needed serving.

"What will you have, Jack?" He asked, putting a Jodi Picoult novel aside.

"A Heineken Zero please, Reg." Jack put one cheek on orangey-brown cloth bar stool. "Can I have a bacon-burger too please?"

“Yessir,” Reg scribbled on a piece of paper and passed it through a narrow hatch behind the bar.

“What’s new?” Clarke asked. “Has the Pope stopped by yet.”

“He has not,” said Reg carefully. “He’s still expected though. But we did have a family of tourists through yesterday. They stopped, as they sometimes do… there’s not a lot else on this road. And their kids weren’t particularly well behaved. You know the type, shoes off, crawling on the floor. But the problem was that the mother started taking pictures. You know how people around here don’t like that.”

“Un-huh,” Jack took a swig of his beer. “I do.”

“It didn’t get any better from there. Some of the boys saw them off. And you know what? They didn’t even pay. That’s annoying for me.”

“People think everywhere is Disneyland. Put there for their entertainment.”

“That’s right! They do. I don’t like that. It hurts business.”

“How is business, Reg?”

He laughed. “I can’t lie, it’s been pretty consistent for a few years now. Not enough to make me a Kardashian, but it’s keeping food in the fridge.”

At least Hazel was a cautious driver. She indicated long before she had to steer the ship into any sudden movements. The roads in her Las Vegas suburb of Enterprise were wide enough to turn an eighteen-wheeler around in. Her house, when they got there, had a double garage as its main feature. Behing the double doors some shapes could be seen to imply that there was a bigger structure, but the drive and garage doors dominated.

Hazel reached over and clawed a door remote out of the glove box. The vehicle had slowed to an almost stop… she pressed the button frenetically, including when the door was already half-way up. Inside was a wide clear landing area. Hanging from the ceiling was a single tennis ball, roughly in the centre of the drive. As she inched the car forward the ball touched the windshield and she stopped the car. Heaving a heavy sigh of relief.

"That's ingenious," Lulu enthused. "What a clever idea."

"Well, it took me one or two drives through the back wall of the garage to come up with the idea." She smiled happily. "Now you two are staying here, you know that?" They nodded carefully. "I told Derek that around here people will sniff you out in minutes if you're anywhere else."

"That's very kind," said Lulu.

"Nonsense," Hazel replied. "I need movement in here to keep the dust down. Now, you two aren't..." She pointed at them meaningfully... "Because I've got you in two rooms."

"Oh! No."

"Nun-uh," came the replies.

"Well, I am a busy old girl myself, so I can't assume others aren't getting busy too." She laughed to herself. They walked through the door from the garage into her living room. "We'll drive up to Silver Peak tomorrow, but for now this is home... but for now I'll get the brandy."

They could hear the car tires and slamming doors before the door at the Old Skool bar opened and a dozen bearded men came in. They were wearing shorts, some in khaki, work boots and dirty, dusty t-shirts. They each had a lanyard in aquamarine with a big plastic pass with a large photo hanging around their neck. Silver Peak Mines, it said on it.

"Hey, Professor, it's Miller Time," said one as he approached the bar with bank card in hand. "Let me have three ice buckets."

“Coming right up,” said Reg, getting to work. Jack put his napkin onto his plate, pushing it away a bit. He pulled out his phone and get scrolling on the bar table. His head turned slightly towards the gathering clan.

“Mitchell! What a stupid fucker,” one was saying.

“What, what happened?”

“He’s gone. He didn’t even make it onto his shift. I suspect he’ll have his car packed and he’ll have left town already.”

“Janey will be sorry.”

“No, she won’t!” They laughed.

“What did he do? What happened?”

“A lighter. He showed up with a lighter in his pocket. It got caught in the metal detector before he even got onto the site. Boom. He’s off. Fired. After, what, almost a year?”

“He started with me… it’s been 10 months. Not that I am counting.” More laughter.

Reg carried the three buckets of ice with bottles of beer in them out to the table. There was a cheer and a few pats on the back for the bartender.

When he got back behind the bar Jack turned to him and said: “Do you get many strangers in here? I don’t mean like the tourists; I mean like me: people who just come and sit and soak it up…”

“Sure. Sure, we do,” Reg replied. “But not always like you. Mostly they’re less subtle than you. It’s clearer they have come here to listen to the boys when they finish their shift.”

Jack tried to hide his surprise. Reg just raised an eyebrow. “Everyone around here knows that lots of people are interested in Silver Peak. It’s like Area 51. But more niche.”

“I’ve been there,” Jack said. Trying to recompose himself. “There are fewer cafés and tourist shops here.”

“Yeah, thank the Lord.”

“So, if there are lots of people with Geiger counters a few hundred miles away in Area 51, what do you get here?”

“Well, like I say, they’re not all like you. But some are. Most people don’t have casual clothes, so they come in in sneakers and Brooks Brothers jackets. Those guys are never from around here. They also leave business cards and ask a lot of questions.” He raised a Tupperware pot of business cards from under the bar. Jack waved it over. “And most of them aren’t American… or if they are, they’re not Nevadans.”

Jack was leafing through the pot. There were car companies: GM, Ford, Toyota, Nissan, Tesla, BMW. But there were also lots of miners: Rio, Vale, Chinalco… and some electronics companies: GE,

Huawei, Apple, MS… It was a Who's Who of the world's plunderer, titans and innovators.

"And what do they do?" Jack asks eventually. "These guys, what do they do?"

"Some just leave. Some corner a guy in the car park and money changes hands."

"And you? Don't they try to cut a deal with you?"

"Yes. Yea. Almost all of them."

"And…?"

Reg smiled. "I already have a state pension." He put down the glass he was drying. "And I know money doesn't come for nothing."

"They must leave stuff behind though… like, I mean…" Jack nodded knowingly.

"Oh, you mean bugs. Yea." Reg pulled out another tub with electronics in it. This one had a lid on it. "I was a Marine. I didn't like it, but I learned a few things…"

Jack let out a low whistle while he inspected the box.

"That's why they should call me The Professor," Reg said.

It wasn't very late, although the sun was definitely thinking of setting. They were seated in Hazel's sunken living room. It had a bit of a Deam Martin vibe. Bamboo chairs shared space with very puffy sofas. Lulu was on the edge of a ratan chair. Bex had almost disappeared into a heavily upholstered chesterfield. They'd had showers and dinner was in casserole pot in the oven. They were now enjoying some more to drink. Tonight, Hazel had broken out the mescal. Bex was feeling warm inside.

Meanwhile, Hazel was warming to the topic of equality and America. "The real problem is that America today has two different tribes in it. Our government at this moment thinks it can boost the economy by regulation. It wants to protect workers and invest in local businesses."

"That's just the way that things were done between the Great Depression and roughly the arrival of Ronald Reagan. In those days both the big US parties believed that the governments job was to keep the playing field level. America was against monopolies. That was a bad word. No one person should hold too much power. Like in Canada and in the UK, we used to try to provide a basic services to all, build highways and drains, and keep people safe."

She paused, but Bex and Lulu were still listening, so she carried on. "Have either of you heard of the Great Compression?" Both of Hazel's guests shook their heads. “Google it sometime,” she laughed and took a great pull off her vape, expelling nothing.

“It was an attempt to keep people and their pay in a narrow band. The idea was to try to avoid extreme poverty, and… extreme wealth.”

“As a result, through, this used to be a fairer country… and by extension… with the same thing happening in other countries… a fairer world. The rising tide raised all boats, as they say.”

Lulu looked a bit perplexed. “We don’t do that now?”

Hazel smiled, stretching her thin lips to create a look that was a bit Muppet-like. “No. Slowly people started saying that approaching things with such a common view was socialism. But they meant communism, because we’d seen what happened in Russia and in some Asian countries, and China was a fright back then.”

“Instead, people argued that *The Market* was key. And it would take care of everything. I remember as a kid we even had board games that suggested this. Market forces, and individual entrepreneurs, would look after the whole economy and make it better for all. Investment from people would expand the economy. Besides this was all about faith in the individual… what could be more American? Everyone is free to chase the American dream.”

Bex nodded.

"But as cities and schools became more exclusive, remote and separate, people started to fear *the other*. People coming to take their money. And who could trust politicians anyway?"

"Today though I see politicians trying once again to hold the economic playing field level, invest in people and in infrastructure to build the economy. And for the past year and a bit, in spite of all the other bad news that's been happening, America is doing okay."

Lulu smiled.

"What's this all got to do with you? And with me, and with Silver Lake?" Hazel asked, although no one had. "You're here, because there are still some people who want to ensure that inequality wins the argument. Ha! Lots of people. And not just countries and so-called State Actors who want to disrupt the balance. But, also, people who have benefitted a lot from the imbalance. There are lots of those, and because money makes you friends, they are still powerful."

"We've met a few," Bexley said. "I've grown up with lots of them, and some days they are me!"

"I've maybe seen it closer than that," Lulu said. "I got my files back from home yesterday. And I made an uncomfortable discovery. I've learned about a family connection that breaks my heart," she said.

“I had an Uncle Jamie who worked in the Foreign Service. He worked as an Economic Attaché to the Canadian Government...”

“So, he was a spy,” Hazel said, with a grin. Lulu paused and then went on.

“He spent time in different parts of the world trying to build my country’s influence. That’s not as you might describe it though, Hazel. As you know, in Canada we tend to be less ambitious ‘Peace, Order and Good Government’ is on the agenda,” she continued.

“But my Uncle Jamie, it turns out paid a lot for his work. He was killed, slowly. His wife first. She was poisoned... leading to diseases and a great deal of discomfort for more than a decade... and Jamie then followed, again through years and years of struggling with poor health.”

“Some of his notes that are in the National Archives suggest he knew who and why his family was being targeted. He named a man called Boa Liang. A Chinese national, and Jamie said, a one-time protégé of his.”

“He’s still alive, that man.” Hazel said with a nod. Lulu nodded too.

“Yes. But his name has changed...”

“Not much,” Hazel laughed.

Bexley looked up. “Is it now Bob Lang?”

"Ding, ding, ding…" Lulu said rocking back in her seat.

Now that they were in a car and moving, Justine took a minute to size up her captor. Jack wasn't as big as he looked from a distance. He was wiry and muscular though. He had a tan that looked like it might never fade. She had recognised his bowlegged gait, and the footsteps that it engendered, from the bunker where she'd been recuperating. He had a nice smile, and thin, wiry, blond-grey hair. She put him at about 60. But he would probably not fear a 20-year-old in a bar fight. And likely take the guy's girlfriend home.

That morning he had brought her the clothes that she had been wearing when she'd disappeared. They were dry-cleaned and hanging under a sheet of plastic. The Target jumpsuits and big-girl pants that she'd been wearing in the bunker she had happily left on the floor.

She knew where they were going, and she was pretty sure she knew why as well. The road to Silver Peak wasn't particularly knowable, but it was perhaps easier to identify by its lack of signs, lights or even a shoulder. There wasn't much traffic up this way.

"What do you do, Jack?" She asked in a perfectly straight way. As if she'd just met him at a cocktail party.

He looked at her sideways without taking his eye off the road. "What do you mean?"

"Well, there aren't enough corporate kidnappings going around these days to keep you busy, are there?" She said while watching the road fly by. "You must have to pick up other jobs here and there. And by the look of you, you have health insurance and somewhere there's a track suit and some runners that you can use to stay fit?"

"I am a civil servant… of sorts."

"Are you saying you're on the government payroll? That seems like a stretch."

"I have been on quite a few government payrolls, if I am honest."

"Often at the same time?"

"I try to avoid that. I am a Refugee Relocation Coordinator."

"Does that mean places like Sierra Leone? Libya? Yemen?" He nodded three times.

"I have been to those places, yes."

"And…?"

"Darfur. Thailand… Mexico. I am less helpful in Africa, I find."

"How about the Uyghurs… you're missing them from your CV," Justine said, trying to rattle him now.

"I'm not actually. I sat that one out. I didn't want to do that." He looked at her for a reaction. "Turning that down wasn't a popular move. I've had to do some things that I wouldn't normally want to as a result." He paused and turned his attention back to the road.

Justine thought for a while. "Do you mean things like what you're doing now?"

"Yea," Jack replied. "This isn't usually my thing. There are plenty of people can do this stuff."

"Should I be complimented? They brought in the professionals?"

Jack smiled. "Just because I say there are lots of people who can do this, doesn't mean that they didn't choose right by getting me involved."

Justine didn't hesitate, "so, then jack. Who is 'they' in this case? It seems to me like they didn't want to kill me. You've been… a… gracious host…"

"Thanks," he smiled and nodded.

"… and you haven't tried to get ,me to tell you anything…"

"I'm not a scientist," Jack said.

"Then why, Jack?"

"Maybe we'll find out shortly…"

Lulu and Bex were each on their own computers in different rooms. Hazel was in the background – listening for sure – and trying to demonstrate a disinterest, but not making too much noise either. Brett Jurys joined the call first, and then the company's security guy.

"There has been some activity," the company guy was saying. "I am not fully at liberty to say what, but, yes, we have seen a few attempts to access company files. They've been easily shut down."

"Can you tell where from? That would be good to know." Brett asked from a fourth screen on the video call.

"No. It has been on a VPN and we can't see that, by definition."

"What about accessing facilities?" Brett asked, "Have you seen any of that happening?"

"Well, no, we have been watching that closely too. There's not been any of that."

"Are you sure that you would know?"

"I *can* tell you that I am looking at a computer now that shows the movements of roughly 33,000 people."

"Yikes," said Bexley. "That's real?"

"Yes," but the man was looking away from his computer. "Hang on, we're seeing something now."

♒

Jack pulled the car alongside one of the vast greenie-blue lakes in Silver Peak. Justine had been staring out the windows in surprise and admiration.

"They're really big, eh?" she said under her breath.

"Yea… it's amazing to me that there are no gates or guards. How do you 'own' this, if anyone can get out and take it as and when they wish? There is miles of lithium here…" Jack asked.

"It's not that easy. This stuff isn't ready to use yet. And it's also not a stable element." She explained. "You can get shovel out and fill the boot of your car… but it's heavy stuff and corrosive over time. If you get it on your skin, it will poison you, slowly."

They got out and walked slowly up to the edge of the briny lake.

"Don't get too close," Justine said. "If you fall in you'd know about it. It's up to 10-feet deep, and near impossible to swim in. You'd not like it."

From over their shoulder they heard the sopund of a car door closing. Justine turned to look. It was really hot. Jack smiled as if he'd been expecting the arrival. Justine turned back to him.

"Are we expecting company?" She asked. Jack walked towards the car.

"You are," he said.

The little car had pulled up, and Justine could see a little man in a big suit stepped out. The heat had already gone right through him. He looked very uncomfortable. His light suit had perspiration marks on it.

"Bob," Jack said with a nod. "Come join us, Justine is about to talk to us about what makes her Lithium so much better than most."

Bob Lang walked uncertainly down the bank of the road towards the lake.

≈

Bexley was in the back again. He was perched with his head poking over the front bench seat of the Cadillac. Hazel was in the passenger seat and Lulu was behind the wheel.

"You can't drive like this in America," Bexley was saying.

"I've taken a defensive driving course," Lulu replied. "And Hazel, I am good for any tickets we get."

"I am sure you are," the old lady replied.

The tickets seemed unlikely. They were on bumpy roads and had been driving a long time. They'd left the US-95 highway recently, They'd been on the road more than three hours from the Las Vegas suburb where Hazel lived. Lulu hadn't slowed the car at all for the bumpy roads.

"There's no one here," she said. "We haven't seen anyone ion half an hour. Hazel? How are you feeling?"

"I'm delighted, dear. I think you can step on it. I don't want to miss the show."

Bob Lang had just been introduced to Justine when they heard a loud noise from up near the road. Lang's car poked over the edge of the highway. Justine, Jack and Bob were standing below it. The lake behind them.

They could hear the wheels spinning of Haxel's Cadillac. The blue of the car contrasted prettily with the lithium lake.

Bob's car started to roll down the hill. Justine and Jack moved to the right. Bob wasn't so fast. The car approached him at speed. He turned and ran into the lake, sloshing up to his knees, before quickly disappearing below the surface. Up on the road Bex and Lulu had gotten out of the car and Hazel had rolled her window down.

"Justine!" Bex shouted. But Jack was pulling her up the bank and they were in the car already. Lulu ran down towards Lang. She stopped at the edge and looked back angrily at Jack and Justine.

Jack stepped on the gas. Then wheels spun and the car disappeared in a cloud of dust.

"Get back in the car Lulu!" Bex said, but she was only walking slowly up the bank again.

"We've lost them," she said with a sigh. The car's bumper is hanging off and we have a flat. "I am *so* sorry Hazel."

"Are you kidding me," the lady replied from the car. "That was awesome! But get back in the car, the air conditioning still works. We'll go find a garage."

"Okay," Lulu said, sticking out her lower lip in disappointment. "Bex you'll have to drive. I'll have to call this one in. We can't just leave this car here and they'll have to fish Lang out."

Bex was horrified. "He's gone? Is there nothing we can do?"

"Well, if we get onto it quickly we can have it cleaned up and avoid some kind of international incident." She laughed to herself. "At least there's no one out here. Maybe we can blame it on the aliens."

It was a short drive to the Old Skool bar. They parked outside and Lulu went in to use the phone. Hazel wasn't going to be left out. But she was shaken. She explained to Bex how to get her mobility scooter out of the back of the car. He set it up and opened the door for her to get onto it.

Together they went into the bar.

Reg greeted them with a nod. It was still early, and shift hadn't ended. Lulu was on the phone.

They took a seat at one of the gnarled tree-trunk tables. Reg appeared with a menu. "Hi Mrs Mayberry," Reg said as he approached their table. "What can I get you all?"

"Two coffees, thanks Reg." Bex looked at the two of them. He shook his head slightly.

Lul came back to the table.

"So, what's the plan now." Bex asked reluctantly. "That simple one doesn't seem to have worked too well."

"The nearest gas station is about an hour away on the 95. They're going to come around." Lulu explained.

"Right," Bex said as the coffees arrived.

"Any food?" Reg asked.

"We'll have a look, thanks Reg," Lulu said.

"You know him too?" Bex asked.

"Yeah," she said. "We just met at the bar. Very friendly people around here."

"I am sorry Nevada hasn't been very nice to you two," Hazel said.

"I like it here." Lulu looked around. "This is my kind of bar. Do you know if they do a karaoke night here, Hazel?" Bex rolled his eyes.

"What will you two do? Do I need to find a way home?" Hazel asked.

"No, my dear," Lulu said. "We're going to loo after you. We need to go back to the airport anyway."

"Where are we going now" Bex asked.

"You and I are going to need to disappear for a while."

Bex's phone beeped. Tickets and an itinerary arrived from Mrs Springer.

Harry Reid was a US senator from Nevada. He'd set up the Senate committee to study UFOs and was always revered in the state for that reason. In 2021 they named the airport after him. The family of his political predecessor, Pat McCarran, were less impressed. The airport had carried his name previously.

Lulu and Bex were in a private plane now, having left Hazel looking wistful, sitting in a mobility scooter on the tarmac. On the way to the airport, they'd learned they were going to Canada. A safe place for most. But even by Canadian standards they were going to a remote location.

"I'm John Hatch," the fair-skinned man had said to Lulu as she followed Bex onto the plane.

"Nice to meet you," she said. "I've heard some things about you. But not too much. Chris isn't really all that talkative."

But now that they were in the air the talk had returned to Silver Peak. The pilot pointed out the vast lakes on the left of then plane as they flew away. Bex and Lulu were both astounded by the lakes. They looked like a used water colour palette. In blues and green and shades that you don't see anywhere else. They could see the gantries that were lined up to slide across the lakes. They presumably were the way that the Lithium was collected off the surface. The vastness of the lakes was amazing to see. Perspective was hard to get, but Hatch pointed out cars by the side of one that looked like tiny specs. Barely distinguishable. They tried to see the wreck of Bob Lang's car that might have been left behind. There was nothing they could see.

"What kind of production does this generate?" Bex asked.

"A lot," Hatch replied.

"Enough to make all the batteries we need?"

"Not yet. No. But it could soon. And thereafter as well. We are looking at plants like this in a few places... not least in Canada," he said looking at Lulu.

"We have some open space available," she replied.

"Yes. You do."

"Why does no one know about this?" Lulu asked. "It seems to be lying out in plain view."

"There are more than a few problems with lithium," Hatch explained. "Although it's pretty from up here, it's very unstable. Once refined it needs to be stored in a vacuum. If it gets shaken about too much it explodes. If you get it on your skin, it burns like hot steel."

"Ouch," said Lulu.

"And all of that makes it far more interesting as a potential target," Hatch continued. "Terrorists. Industrial espionage."

"Foreign countries," Bex added. "Like our friend Mr Lang?"

"I know that's what you guys have some recent experienced with, yes. But it's often domestic terrorists that the Americans have to worry about."

"What, why?" Bex asked.

"Well, there are more of them. They get around the USA more easily."

"But why would they want to target this place? It seems like somewhere people wouldn't know about, or care about."

"You'd think so," Hatch said. "But it's not like that. People in the USA are often looking for new ways to get people's attention. And there are many, many places you can get a list of American 'strategic assets'. This place is always on those lists."

Bex wasn't convinced. "But what would they hope to do by attacking this place? It seems out of the way and innocuous."

"'Out of the way' is definitely one of the good things about it. It's a harder target when you can't approach it un-observed. But still there are people who would try. And there was of course that Chinese balloon earlier this year. I bet someone didn't get paid their bonus for that idea."

"I still don't see who would want to upset something that is addressing our power issues. This place is helping us save the planet, no?" Chris wasn't convinced.

"Yes, but to some people it might also represent progress," Hatch explained. "Or technology. Or environment distress. Or the 'military industrial complex'. It's increasingly hard to keep track of what people are protesting against. It changes and there are people against most things. I think it's more fun to be against something than to be for it."

"You should have chatted to Hazel," Lulu said dryly.

"Oh, don't worry, I have spoken to Hazel a lot. She's a bit of a legend in our business," and he winked awkwardly at Lulu.

"Help me, Johnny," Bex interjected. "Just what the hell is your business?"

Hatch just smiled.

Lulu was clearly more game. "We're spies," she said enthusiastically. "Like the ones on TV. Except we actually have to drive, or bus, or fly to places.

We can't magically appear. Oh, and we go to the bathroom too."

"And we don't get to drive motorcycles through a souk," Hatch agreed.

"Oh, but we could," Lulu laughed.

The flight turned slightly right as they reached Salt Lake City.

Chapter 7 – Disappear

Flow

The psychologist Mihály Csíkszentmihályi must have struggled to get his name printed on the back of his football jersey. But his views on the state of being have been important for business theorists. What we used to call 'being in the zone, he refers to as 'flow'. First presented in 1970, Csíkszentmihályi describes it as being physically and mentally caught up in what one is doing – in such a way that creates a positive feeling and causes time to lose its relevance. Csíkszentmihályi explained that humans are exposed to about 110 pieces of information per second. Flow allows you to shut those out and really focus on one thing. It is an active state of being. However, he also explains that it needs to be productive. It is not something you find while sitting in a bath or daydreaming on a bus. It necessarily involves the achievement of some desirable results. While there is an obvious application to education, theorists have also tried to understand it in the world of sports, music, design, and everyday white-collar office work.

♒

The plane touched down at Mont-Joli airport without incident. The little town on the south shore of the St Lawrence River in Quebec has an airport that can take a 747 – although it rarely does. Unlike Gander airport in Newfoundland, it didn't collect trans-Atlantic flights on September 11th. But it could have.

During the second world war, allied pilots were sent to Mont-Joli to practice their aerial bombardment. Boats towed targets out into the sea and pilots were given two distinctive houses on the coast to use for triangulation. The training was immensely useful. Unfortunately, the local graveyard includes the war graves of a few pilots from places like New Zealand and Norway, proving that even practice was not without its risks.

A car met Bex and Lulu at the foot of the plane's stairs. It was mild but warm enough for summer. There was a sea smell in the air and the air felt soft. Hatch explained what was going to happen next and thanked them before getting back on the plane. They opened the door to the car and saw there was someone already in it.

"Tristan?" Chris said doubtfully.

"It is I!" Hope-Hartley said. "Do get in. Hello, Lulu, we haven't met."

"What are you doing here?" Bexley demanded, "I thought you were retired."

"Yes. Retired, mate, but not dead. I know a few people and they know a few people and here I am. Get in, we have some road to do."

They put their bags, such as they were, in the trunk, and settled in.

"Lulu, have you ever been to Cacouna before?" the retired English banker asked the younger Canadian.

"I have not." She replied. "But I have studied it in history class. The Canadian cabinet met there at least once, no?"

"They did," he said proudly. "Good knowledge."

"That's all I've got though."

"I will be happy to tell you more, but let me first tell you my favourite Canadian politic story..."

"You have one," Bex said incredulously.

"Mate, I do. I know some stuff. There was a fellow called John A Macdonald who was Canada's first Prime Minister." Lulu nodded her approval. "And his great nemesis was the Whig called George Brown. And John A also had a bit of a drink problem. This bit is not taught in Social Studies class. He used to have the page boys bring glasses of pure vodka to him in the Houses of Parliament. One day after George had given Macdonald and his government a severe tongue-lashing on the floor of the house

Macdonald rose unsteadily to his feet and promptly vomited all over his desk."

"Oh!"

"And he looked up at Brown and said 'I often feeling like doing that when the Honourable Gentleman speaks.' "

"Excellent," said Lulu.

Cacouna is a summer resort town of the kind that is hard to find in other countries. There's a bit of New England summer retreat to it, and a bit Nordic seaside village. But it is different to those places too.

Although Cacouna was settled as a fishing settlement the great and the good had been buying up the land, building clapboard houses and flocking there for about 150 years. There was an 18-hole golf club, 10 tennis courts and a clapboard club house that served no real purpose except to show films and host the summer Dinner Dance.

Cacouna boasted large, summer-only houses lining its stony beach. The nicer houses had paths down to the water. Some with hidden kayaks and canoes, but for the most part the river was only to look at here. It is 40 miles wide, strongly tidal and really,

really cold. Even in the dead of summer, the salt-water 'river' was just a scenic backdrop. An ocean that felt less vast.

Tristan took them to hi family 'compound'. The Hartley Compound. It was not on the water but set back from the rest of the settlement, removed and happy about it. There were three houses on the property. Although not lined up, they were each smaller than the one before. The third was really just a posh shed.

Bex and Lulu were going to be dropped in the middle house. A cottage, by local parlance. Tris would be in the posh shed. Their host, Tristan's second cousin, had the run of the main house and was conveniently away for the week. But not convenient enough to let them sleep in the larger bedrooms. They were, nonetheless, going to be using his liquor cabinet.

Bexley felt comfortable even as they alighted from the plane. There was lovely sea air. It was cool. But not cold. The houses along the road that they drove to Cacouna were not all well-kept. But there was a quiet dignity to the place, even though it was most likely a hard place to live in the winter. Little roadside canteens had signs advertising lobster suppers. There were signs signalling snowmobile crossings, and there were fishing nets and lobster traps drying in some yards. But there were also above-ground pools, large car dealerships, and chain stores.

Bex and Lulu had received instruction from Tristan. Thery were there to lay low. So, there was no golf or tennis in their future. But they could shower, change, and meet their host on the main house's terrace where he would be serving drinks. Dinner would be prepared in their house while they had cocktails. No one would cross paths.

Bexley walked up the steps uneasily in the best clothes he could muster. He heard the clinking of ice and could see Lulu already seated in the soft light of the sun setting over the far side of the river. He felt good.

"Tell us some things we need to know, Tris," Bex said as they were all seated looking out to sea.

"That would be hard, as I don't know much about what you two are up to." He held up his hand. "And I would rather not too. What can I tell you about *international finance*...?" He looked discouraged as he said it. But Lulu jumped in.

"Tell us about China," she said. "What is going on there now, and why would they want things that we have, like, say, lithium...?"

Tristan Hope-Hartley crossed and uncrossed his legs. The red trousers still looked well ironed. He shook his drink a bit and stood to top everyone up. Then he started to talk.

"Okay, let's talk about China. Things aren't going particularly well in the People's Republic at the moment. Xi Jinping has had a good run. He's been the boss for more than a decade and the country has largely gone from strength to strength. But some cracks are starting to show. That might explain the Lithium thing, but let me come back to that."

"There's a youth unemployment problem. Quite a big one. Almost 20% of young people are out of work. That's one in five. Or they were last time data was published. The Party didn't like what it was seeing... so... they... stopped publishing the data. In the big cities now young people are being offered jobs at about $2.50 an hour. That compares to the minimum wage of £10 in the UK and, I think, about $16 in Canada. You might say that the cost of living should be cheaper there... in China, but it's not. In these megacities, you can't live on $2.50 an hour. Not even close."

"On top of that, they have had a massive real estate bubble – which has just gone; Pop! The Party had encouraged house building. They had bankrolled it and helped people to buy..."

"Evergrande? Bex added.

"Correct," said Tristan. "That was a $300billion black hole. They had thousands of developments underway in hundreds of cities."

"Meanwhile China's own technology miracle has started to lose air. They have saturated their own economy and have limits on what they can do elsewhere. Tech companies are laying people off. And not just anyone. They're laying off people with master's degrees. The Party knows that this is a big risk. They are sowing the seeds of their own undoing. They have over-promised. There are lots of people with money in China now. They have 10% of the world's millionaires. People know what money can buy. And they've been led to believe they should be able to buy it."

"Is this making sense?"

"Yes," said Bex. "Very helpful," he added politely.

"Meanwhile Xi and his mates have been out spending the money that they thought they'd always have. They have this programme with the pedestrian name of the Belt and Road Initiative. To be honest most governments in the West have been wringing their hands about it."

"I'll admit that it never seemed that clever to me, but what do I know. I'm just a money guy."

"The Belt and Road Initiative is this massive international push by China to give tied-loans to so-called developing nations around the world. In other words, we will give you the money now, but you need to spend it with us, and then pay us back for the pleasure of doing that."

“And China hasn’t just been doing this here or there. They have invested in 150 countries, on every continent. Not surprisingly, there’s been very little in western Europe, or North America. Brazil has also been a hold out. They’ve not taken much Chinese money. Even though some political leaders ask why.”

“Xi started this the year after he came to power. They have been building high-speed trains in Africa, they’ve invested in infrastructure like ports and roads… they’ve built power plants, highways, airports, telecommunications networks and other infrastructure. They’ve brought in Chinese engineers and project managers, and in some cases Chinese labour… and then offered the countries financing so they could pay China back later.”

“Most of these countries, perhaps more savvy than we give them credit for, took the money while they could. In total Xi and the Chinese government have spent close to $1 trillion on the Belt and Road Initiative. That’s a little more than the whole GDP of Switzerland. That’s a lot of money.”

“And it has just started to become clear to them now, that they’re not going to get much of that back. Let alone back-with-interest.”

“Meanwhile, they’re discovering the hard way that you can’t simply buy influence. The diplomatic alliances that they saw coming naturally out of their great generosity… aren't materialising. You've got to build trust if you want to make a real, long-term relationship. My first boss in banking taught me that."

"Interesting," said Bex.

"Sobering," Lulu said.

The sun had set, they had eaten their dinner, and there was a chill in the air now. They each headed off to bed.

♒

"Chris, where are you?" Against his better judgment Bexley had agreed to take a video call from Brett Jurys. "What's that weird carving behind you?" He hadn't thought of the folk art as a potential give-away. He turned the screen slightly.

"I've had to disappear for a while. What's on your mind Brett? I don't think I should be talking to you right now. I'm meant to be laying low."

"Okay, I will be fast. I need to tell you something. It's not going to look good on me. But maybe you can find some way to not make me feel more guilty."

"Okay, Brett, I am listening. Tell me more."

"I am responsible for Justine's disappearance."

"Sorry? You abducted her? She's with you?"

"No, no, nothing like that. But I might as well have. You see we still have a shared calendar. It's been necessary for managing the kids and… even when you're separated, you're not actually separated, you're just like, still in business together."

"Okay. I follow."

"I got to talking to a guy through work recently he represented a potential overseas partner. He was going to invest quite a lot of money in my business. It would have been a game-changer. And then one day he asked about Justine, he'd heard she was going to be abroad and said they had a friend in common. So, I told him where she was staying… I might have even mentioned the room number…"

"Okay," said Bex. "That's not great. I get that. What was the trip? Was it Philadelphia?"

"It was," Brett said, with real remorse in his voice. "it was the Four Seasons."

"Right, well, that's life, Brett. Listen, that's not as bad as you think. If it hadn't been you, it would have been someone else, or they might have hacked your system… tell me though, who was this guy? Does he have a name?"

"Yes, but I've tried to reach him, and I can't find him anymore. He's disappeared."

"And…"

"He's called Bob Lang."

"Oh, yes. Of course," Bex said.

"You know him?" Brett asked.

"I knew him… he died a few days ago."

The books on offer in this little house in Quebec were not all Booker Prize winners. Lulu had settled on a hard-cover tome called *Gracefully Insane* about a mental hospital for the very wealthy in a suburb of Boston. She found it very diverting. But she was struggling to stay off of her technology. They'd been told to be sparing in its use. Electronic breadcrumbs and all that. Their evening with drinks and sunsets were the highlights of what were becoming increasingly long days.

"I've done a bit more research, I might have made a little call or two…" said Tristan as they assembled on their second night on the porch of the big house.

"What's tonight's topic, Professor Hartley?" Lulu enthused.

"That's Hope-Hartley, Miss. The double-barrel is important where I come from."

"Yessir," she said. "For me too."

"Tonight's topic is Lithium." He looked at piece of paper in his hand. "Known as 'LI' in the periodic table. It has an atomic number of 3. Most people have never really given it much thought. It's used in atomic bombs but not in great quantity. But then we had to find a way to store energy when this whole 'climate crisis' who-ha came along…" Lulu rolled her eyes at him.

"Lithium is now very important for many reasons. Last November it would have cost you $60,000 a tonne. Today it's closer to $40k. But that's still a lot. You could buy a lot of gold for that money. And a lot of soybeans too, for that matter."

"But lithium is special and it's special to us too. It's hard to mine, hard to store, and hard to transport. Although apparently the stars are full of it. But lithium is needed now more than ever… Demand is expected to grow about 30% a year for at least the next ten years."

"And do you know who will need the most of it?"

Lulu put up her hand like schoolgirl. "I'm going to guess China," said Bex.

"That is right, mate. Then Europe… then the United States. So, although China is producing more lithium than anyone else right now, it cannot sustain that position. Even though its demand is growing faster than anyone else's. That's a rotten position for the Party to find themselves in. On top of that the Chinese economy generally is headed in the wrong direction. While other world economies are starting to pick up. The Chinese are not particularly fond of the Russians. They don't like expansionist countries. But they also have a 4,000-kilometre shared border with Russia. That's about 2,500-miles, in real money."

"China has a good history in working with raw minerals, but most of the innovation these days still comes from away. They buy it in from Australia, the US, or Japan. Although the relationships between China and those other countries are still a bit chilly. But lithium isn't iron ore. You can't ship it around in a crate and leave it sitting on a dock somewhere."

"So, this is a diplomatic issue as well?" Lulu asked.

"It sounds like there's some industrial espionage at work," Bex added.

"That's right, mate. The Chinese know they have a lithium problem and they're panicking," Tristan said. "Their great venture into real estate has just gone sideways. They need more lithium and they need it now. Sooner rather than later. And they need – to go along with that – the skills and tech required to manage it."

"That's going to be harder to come by," he concluded.

The warm air felt familiar to Justine when the airplane doors opened. She knew intuitively that it wasn't China, but it was awfully close. Jack picked up her bag and pointed her towards the door. Although they were in what was called a Special Administrative Region, everyone knew what that really meant. This was China by default.

The sprawling city was now disappearing into the surrounding peninsulas, valleys, coves and bays around the area. One could easily disappear here. One of the highest density areas of human habitation in the world. People disappeared here all the time.

Jack ordered people around in what sounded like a very convincing Mandarin. It even sounded like he was gossiping with the driver now. That's some kind of Refugee Programme, Justine thought.

They drove through the city. It was evening now, but the lights were on in every shop and strung through the streets. Justine had been to Hong Kong before, but not in a few years. It had always had an edge. You can't have that many people rubbing up against each other without some kind of friction. But owe she sensed an added hesitation. She had a feeling that there was more danger to be found here now. People walked quickly with their heads down.

If China has caught a cold, then Hong Kong was feeling pretty achy too.

By the third day Tristan said he had a surprise for his fellow refugees. They were going to the July "Dinner Dance" at the sports club. It was a costume party and Bex and Lulu were warned not to talk to deeply to anyone, or risk bringing attention to their situation and threats to themselves. The theme was going to be "The 1980s – come as you were or as you wanted to be".

Lulu was delighted. Bex was less convinced.

They agreed to look through closets and meet up ready to go on the porch at 6pm.

Tristan was there first already looking very pleased with himself. He had on some leather trousers, a head band and a fake handle-bar moustache. "I'm a hair-rocker," he said proudly.

"Let me guess, Lulu, you are a Material Girl…?"

"Yes," she replied. "Not totally my era, but there's a simplicity to just putting your bra on over your top."

"You're doing okay," he said.

"Okay, let's go," said Bex as he approached. But Lulu and Tristan exchanged a glance and turned together to look. Bexley was wearing running shoes, jeans with turned up cuffs, a dress shirt, a puffy orange gilet, sunglasses and carrying a skateboard.

“Brilliant.”

“Great Scott!“ Tristan shouted.

“What’s a flux capacitor, Doc?” said Lulu.

The dinner dance was a success.

“Do you know anyone here?” Bexley asked Lulu when they met up briefly during the outdoor drinks party before the dinner.

“Are you kidding me? Almost everyone here works with me,” she replied, as she nodded almost imperceptibly to another reveller.

Bex found that he could slowly get into the groove of things. The establishment accepted bank cards, even from the UK, so he asked the pre-teen tending his table to keep the wine bottles coming. He bid on pieces of driftwood in the silent auction. And was unsure what he would do with a week at a house for 12 in South Carolina this winter, but he bid on it and won.

Slowly they started clearing the tables and the music began. Somehow it seemed to land just right. Mr Brightside by the Killers. Blue Monday by New Order. Bex didn't think he knew these things. He was amazed by Lulu's dancing. All arms and legs, she was somewhere between a traditional Russian folk dancer and a bug pinned to a corkboard.

To Lulu, Bex was the best dancer she had seen in a while. She stared at him in awe. He barely moved, just an arm drawing a line or knees moving side to side in unison, like David Byrne. They danced away the alcohol – or at least the water part of the alcohol – through perspiration.

At one point Tristan tapped Bex on the shoulder and explained that he was going home. He'd see them in the morning. Bex waved him off with a flourish that was more Mr Bean than the Court of Louis XIV.

Eventually the lights came up. And Lulu was walking beside him down the street with her shoes in her hand.

Then suddenly they were horizontal. Home and in Lulu's bed. At some point she had put a tensor bandage on her knee. "It'll hurt in the morning otherwise." And Bex could feel the heat of her thighs pressing up against his face. When he'd started, her legs were cool and soft. But now he could hear two hands hitting the mattress. One was Lulu's as the noises she was making increased in both frequency and volume. The other was Chris' free hand. He was trying to get some grip, or at least get her attention, as he felt the strength of her muscles flexing around his head.

More than 12,000 kilometres away John Hatch alighted from a British Airways plane at Chek Lap Kok airport. He stood in the queue for immigration, British passport in hand. As he approached the gate he caught a familiar figure out of the corner of his eye. Passing between two curtains in the secure customs area he thought he recognised the hunched figure of Bao Liang. He knew Liang was old, he was a legend in security circles. He'd been in the field for so long. But this version was different. The man's hair was missing, his skin was covered in rashes. It looked like acne. He was shaking – tremors. But then he was gone. Hatch was sure his information suggested that Lang was a casualty of the trip to Silver Peak.

Hatch had been trained in observation skills. But he'd not spent much time actually in the field for many years – over a decade really – so he doubted his own eyes. He quietly reprimanded himself and put it down to a profiling error that he'd rather not think about.

♒

Tristan said nothing when he came to the little house to wake Chris and Lulu. They emerged sheepishly, and there was a certain tension in the air.

"I'm sorry to say you need to go now," he said while he looked around for any of their belongings, he could help them pack. "Take it," he said, handing Lulu her book.

"You both need to be in Mont-Joli and in the air as quickly as possible. It seems like everyone you are looking for is assembling now… on the other side of the planet."

"Dammit," said Lulu, scooping up her mobile phone from a corner table in the front room. "They tell me not to use my phone, and then all hell break loose."

"Where are we going?" Bex asked putting a kettle on.

"You're headed to Hong Kong… And there will be coffee on the plane." He picked up a bag and held the front door of the house open.

"You'll have to connect through Vancouver. It's going to be a long trip."

Chapter 8 – Central

Daniel Goleman and Emotional Intelligence

Raised in California, both of Goleman's parents were university lecturers. He was surrounded by smarts. But it was his travels in India on a Harvard fellowship that are mostly cited as cause for his most famous theory. A PhD in psychology, Goleman became a popular columnist and commentator, writing for the New York Times for more than a decade. When he was almost 50 years old his third book Emotional Intelligence: Why It Can Matter More Than IQ *became an international bestseller. He explained that emotional intelligence, or 'EQ', had four basic components: self-awareness, self-management, social awareness, and relationship management. The term has now passed into the business and human resources vernacular. It now appears in all the major English-language dictionaries.*

The Central District Police Headquarters in Hong Kong looks like it could be a regional hospital in the UK, or a refugee centre in the US. It is a modular high-rise. As a result it doesn't lend itself architecturally to cooperation and coordination between people. It is possible for people, who are meant to be on the same team, not to see each other at all.

On top of that, the local police have been perhaps the hardest hit by the slow reunification with China. Their instructions are often contradictory, and their occasional lapses get more scrutiny than in the People's Republic. Western media loved reporting on errors made by the Hong Kong police. It was a hard job. There were many ways of approaching it.

Derek 'Killer' Cahill seemed to have made friends with some people who were interested in his cooperation. That's how he, Lulu and Bex came to be in a windowless room at the back of the fourth floor in the 'International' unit.

"That's it," said Cahill as he pushed the camera away to point at a wall, and switched off the wide-screen TV. "We have some level of agreement. I think we should be happy about that."

"That wasn't as easy as it should have been." Bexley slumped a bit in his chair, pushing it back to get more legroom.

"Maybe you're not cut out for policework, Chris," Cahill said sympathetically.

"I *definitely* am not," the Englishman said. "I really like my job. I sit around a lot. I drink a lot of coffee and eat a lot of pastries…"

Lulu laughed. But Cahill got there first: "Well, in that case, I take it back, maybe you are cut out for this!"

♒

"Elizabeth Holmes!" Justine shouted. Pleased with herself, but also aware that she was still a bit groggy. "She's the one I have been trying to ma'member. She's in jail now. I am pretty sure." She bent her head a bit and mumbled. "Poor Elizabeth."

"Take some more coffee, Justine." Jack instructed, shaking her coffee thermos. "Finish this and I will make you some more. I don't want to have to give you a shot of adrenaline."

"And Amanda Knox! What ever happened to her?! She seemed okay. A bit naughty, but okay." She paused. "Jack? Jack! I think we could have been friends... Betsy, Knoxy and me."

"Justine, you need to drink up. Of all the things I wanted to hear from you, this was not on the list. I think you need to get up and walk around..." He slung her arm over his shoulder and marched her around the suite. They stopped at the window and they both looked out. Then they kept walking. The lights of the Central District of Hong Kong twinkled below. The Star Ferries, reassuringly lit up, could be seen moving around the water.

Bex was shaking his head. Lulu had just retrieved six sheets of paper from the printer and she was stapling the top right corner. Killer Cahill was holding a brown envelope open.

"You really think this will work?" Chris asked.

"Why not?! Are you questioning the great breakthrough of William J Plunkett in 1938?" Lulu said with a smile. "I don't think Bill would be pleased with you."

Bexley continued, "I appreciate that you've edited the text – a bit – and changed the masthead, but the article is about the making of Teflon, not..."

"It's called Polytetrafluoroethylene, Chris," she said, while sealing the paper in the envelope, "and the Journal of the American Chemical Society is a respected publication."

"But it's almost 100 years old. No one is going to believe that..."

Cahill joined in. "They don't really have to, though, do they. There won't be the time for detailed assessments."

"That's what you hope," said Bexley.

On the eastern part of the site of the old city hall is the old Bank of China building. You can find similar buildings in cities connected to Britain all over the world. Two dragons still sit outside the door of this early 'skyscraper'. Its main lobby is a celebration of art deco glory.

Discrete visitors will make a bee-line for the lifts and head for the top three floors where The China Club resides. The 13th floor is home to the popular Michelin-starred restaurant, still only accessible by paying members and their guests. (Roughly $20,000 will get you a membership.) The 14th floor is home to Long March Bar, and the 15th floor – the very top of the white stone building – houses some private rooms, mostly used for card games and mah-jong.

Bex, Lulu and Cahill were trying to look the part when they entered the lift and pressed 15. Some were more successful than others. Cahill's black running shoes kind of gave the game away, but he was styling it out... or so he felt. Chris had told him he looked like Jimmy Nail in *Spender*. He assumed the reference would be lost on him, but Killer was delighted. That had caused Bexley some alarm.

Chris knew that both Cahill and Lulu were carrying guns. He'd never been keen on guns, avoiding them at all costs. But he was also fascinated to see they hadn't faced any challenge at all on leaving the hotel, entering the police station or travelling into one of Hong Kong's grandest private members clubs. Clearly Hong Kong today was a different kind of place.

When the lift doors opened on the top floor, there were six doors to choose from. The grandest of the lot has a paper sign on it saying: "Greenstuff Capital". That felt a bit clunky, Bex thought, as they pushed through the door, but he decided to keep that to himself.

"Johnny Heck!" Bexley shouted as soon as he was in the room.

"Bex! You're still alive?" John Hatch said in reply. Although with a warm smile.

"Time will tell…" he said ruefully. "Tell me how is it that you always seem to appear where I am. You must have some amazing air miles."

"I am much less mobile than you are, Bex. Do you even know what day it is?"

"Only when these two tell me," he nodded towards his two colleagues.

"Lulu," he shook her hand. "Derek," he addressed Cahill and gave him a quick man-hug.

Justine and Jack arrived about 5 minutes later. Jack spoke in Mandarin to a man who appeared by the lift. Then Jack directed the Mining CEO towards a lift that said 'Out Of Order' on the door. It opened and they stepped in.

The muzak played an electric symphonic version of Carly Rae Jepsen's *Call Me Maybe*. Justine tapped her foot. "Stop that!" said Jack.

They alighted on the 14th floor and walked up the stairs to the 15th. Jack opened the door gingerly and then crossed and pushed through the door marked for some finance company. He held Justine in front of him, close and she could feel a lump of cold metal near the middle of her back. Still in its holster, on the right side of his body.

Bexley, Cahill and Lulu were all sitting at one of the two cocktail tables that made up the total furnishings of the room. There were three high stools that they were perched on. The three of them turned and greeted the new arrivals with a smile.

"Justine."

"Jack."

"Jack."

"You're not entirely within your jurisdiction here, Jack, are you?" Cahill said, lightly.

"Neither are you, 'Killer'," Jack replied equally lightly. A wind rustled through the open doors onto the glass balcony. Hong Kong's asymmetrical Stonehenge of high-rises lay around them. Stars and a moon could just be glimpsed between them.

"This is fun. What are we here for again?" Lulu said. "Oh, yeah. It's international espionage night."

"Wait, you're a spy?" said Bex with mock incredulity.

"I just need the document." Jack said quietly. "Then you can all be off. And go home to wherever you come from."

"We're all refugees, Jack," Lulu chimed in. "We're awaiting relocation."

"Do you have what you have been asked for or not?"

Cahill held up the brown envelope. "How do you pronounce it? *Holstey-UM*? Or is it more Hole-*steam*? Justine? You invented it, maybe you can tell us?"

The door behind Jack and Justine opened and a very unwell Bao Liang rolled in. The behind him man pushing his wheelchair wore a brown Homburg and an expression of great concentration. Both hands were guiding the wheelchair. Liang had lost most of his hair and aged significantly. His skin had broken out like a teenager. There was a gun on his lap.

"Bob?" Cahill said. "What the hell has happened to you?" backing slightly towards the corner of the room Jack stepped back to have a look, keeping Justine close to him.

"Lithium," said Bob Lang or Bao Liang. "It is ironic, I know ... I don't know. I think the English expression is 'hoisted by my own petard', correct?"

Bex laughed involuntarily.

"I'm ready to retire anyway. I've had enough," Bob lang said unconvincingly.

His awkwardly fitting suit, normally a size too large for him, looked like it was crafted for a much bigger man.

"If heaven made me, then the earth can find some use for me," said Bob.

'Pop!' Cahill raised his hand above the table and shot the man in the Homburg hat in the right shoulder. The man slumped to the ground, unable to reach inside his coat with his right hand to get his gun under his left arm.

Bao Liang reached down and lifted his gun in a shaking hand. Jack took three big steps across the room while Bex, Killer and Lulu instinctively ducked behind the cocktail table. Jack Clarke pulled the gun out of the old man's grip.

Sensing a moment Justine grabbed the envelope off the table where Cahill had abandoned it and made her way to the balcony. She hung her arm with the Holstium recipe over the railing. They were fifteen storeys up and the wind was circling.

“Hang on,” everyone just calm down,” Jack shouted as he took cover behind the old man and his wheelchair. A gun in hand. Lulu, Bex and Cahill watched carefully from the side. Inactive spectators.

There was a long pause. No one moved. You could hear a few people breathing.

“Christ, Lang!” Jack suddenly said. “Have you pissed yourself? That’s disgusting, man.”

“It’s not me. It’s the lithium. It’s the Party’s work!”

“So, what happens now?” Cahill shouted from under the table.

But another window crashed before the words had travelled around the room. Jack dropped his gun and grabbed his right arm with his left. Justine lifted both her hands to her head and slid down the wall. The envelope ended up in her lap. John Hatch appeared through the main door and walked over, kicking Jack’s gun away. The three spectators stood up and looked around. “Blimey! What the heck is going on?” said Bex.

But Jack pushed Liang’s wheelchair forcefully towards the balcony, and scrambled out the door. Cahill, Hatch, Lulu and Bex rushed after him..

Boa Liang looked up and brought his chair to a slow stop, he leaned forward carefully and slowly to pick up the brown envelope by Justine's feet. She reached slowly over to the wheel of his chair and rolled him carefully through the adjacent, broken glass balustrade. He made no sound as he fell. The wheelchair descended at a different speed to the street below. The brown envelope fluttered down behind him.

Jack was once again into the out-of-service elevator and gone. Cahill pressed the elevator button frantically. Hatch ran to the stairs and was gone. Lulu and Bex looked at each other helplessly. The bell rang and an elevator door opened. They all climbed in.

At the base of the building when Jack came out of the elevator a man was standing just along the pavement holding an electric bicycle for him. There was a disturbance on the other side of the building and all attention seemed to be focused there. Bob Lang had woken up the city, as a final act. Sirens could be heard in the background. Casually Jack said a few words to the man, took the electric cycle, stepped on to it and disappeared into the traffic on Des Voeux Road.

The man walked away quietly.

Moments later the building doors opened again. Killer, Bexley and Lulu came out. They looked around frantically. But stopped suddenly when they heard a loud bang from the direction of the harbour. The e-bike had exploded. They saw a big flame, then a cloud of smoke, which lingered a while.

Epilogue – Deduction

Aristotle's logic

It can be hard to agree what we really know about the Greek polymath. He lived in the fourth century BC. Likely for about 60 years. He studied under Plato and tutored the son of Alexander the Great. We now have gathered what is believed to be only about a third of his total output. He is credited with some of the earliest studies of logic. His contributions to modern science have had a long-term impact right up to today. In management he developed the simple process of deduction. For example, all men are mortal, all Greeks are men, therefore all Greeks are mortal.

♒

Christopher Bexley stepped out of his car onto the streets of Cambridge. His youngest daughter Fleur's summer term was coming to an end. She was now going to be working in London for a term, at a hedge fund, and living at home again.

He found her sitting on her bags in the quad.

"Papa!" she said as she threw her arms around him. "How are you? I am so happy to see you. I am tired. It's been a long term and last night was an even longer celebration. I am bit jaded."

"We will get you home, young woman," Chris assured her. "There is food and your bed is made up and we will have a good autumn together, you and I."

"Yes, I am excited Popa. Life must be so boring for you, all on your own these days," she stuck out her lower lip. "I am here though, I will make it exciting."

"Oh, no. You don't have to do that," he said over his shoulder as he headed for the car carrying two huge bags.

♒

"She'll see you now," the handsome young assistant said, as he held the door open for Bexley at the top of the low-rise glass tower near the London Wall.

He walked through the door and across the hall into Justine's office. She looked at her watch and stood up. "So, it's 10 am already, is it? Hello, Chris, how nice to see you! In real life, as well. What a nice change."

"I am trying, Madame Chair, I am trying," Chris said shaking his head. "But I think we'll still do video sessions, if we are to keep working together.

I'll do what you tell me Chris. I don't know how we got through the summer, but I sure do appreciate your help."

Lulu stopped at the newsstand just off the Sparks Street Mall in Ottawa. She reached into the racks and pulled out a copy of the South China Morning Post. "Chinese economy suffers from real estate collapse", said the main headline. "New deal for Africa", it said below, talking about another future mining agreement signed recently. This time in Chad. The accompanying photo showed six men standing stiffly. No one was smiling. Down at the bottom of the page was a series of short "INSIDE" stories. One dealt with a possible ban of recycled batteries on electric bikes and scooters. The Government of the SAR of Hong Kong was looking into it.

Lulu paid for the paper with her card and walked out into the sunshine.

Car batteries could change forever with Toyota breakthrough in solid state tech

26 October 2023

Toyota claims may soon be able to mass produce a solid-state battery. The announcement could upend the electric car industry.

That means that in the near future EVs of could achieve ranges of more than 700 miles on a single charge. They say charging time could shrink, with a full charge taking just 10 minutes.

The End

Acknowledgements

Thank you for making it this far. Indeed, thank you for buying this book.

I write for therapy. I am a pathological communicator. I enjoy writing and this the second 'Christopher Bexley' book once again allows me to go places and spend time with people I find interesting and – mostly – amusing.

If it touches on ideas or issues that make you think, then more the better. I've left something on you.

DID3826703
L - #0098 - 100124 - C0 - 203/127/10 - PB - DID3826703